BRUTAL
HEIR

BRUTAL HEIR

COURT UNIVERSITY: BOOK ONE

EDEN O'NEILL

PROLOGUE

Greer - age 9

I got sick on my shorts. Hunkering down, the harsh smell twisted my stomach again, my hands on my shaking legs. The bite on my ankle oozed blood, and I brought my leg in, cradling it as I listened for sounds. Some rustling behind me and I was on the ground, hugging my knees and hoping the dog couldn't find me. Old Man Peabody let it out again.

Oh, God. Oh, God. Please.

Movement behind me and I was almost sick again, trembling as I eased a look behind the tree that hid me. The dog had chased me for nearly ten minutes, exhaustion quivering my limbs as much as the fear. When I saw nothing, I was up, running again as fast as I could. I found another tree and I hugged it.

It was all quiet.

Too quiet, I closed my eyes, listening. The animal cry made me jump, the yelp right after shooting a harsh sense of fear inside me. The struggled cry had sounded like a dog, the yelp the same.

More rustling and movement in the leaves beneath my feet sounded. I left the tree, escaping its security to find two local boys. They were hunkered over something, and both were familiar to me. The one with the blond hair and light-colored eyes liked to play with the master of the house my mom cleaned and cooked for. His name was Royal, and he held down something, his hands white and knuckled over fur.

They no longer knuckled as I got closer, no longer needed. The thing below him wasn't moving. He sat back on his haunches, staring up at the other boy there. He was the master of the house with his grandfather, only a couple years older than me and the boss of my mom, who was an adult. I hadn't known kids could be in charge until I met him, moved into his house with my mom.

A twig snapped under my sneaker, and that boy gazed up at me, eyes a coal black even from here, though I knew them to be brown. I stared at him a lot when he couldn't see, dark and harsh and angry, always angry. A sweep of dark hair breezed across his forehead, shielding eyes that bored into me. Some of that anger descended my way, dark eyebrows above like storm clouds.

Knight Reed wet his lips, a rock raised above his head. Frozen, he stared at me, the thing dripping red onto the mass of fur on the ground below him. Backing away, Royal put space between himself and the scene, but Knight hadn't moved. He stayed, watching me, and closer now, I saw what he hovered over. Before I had met Old Man Peabody's dog, I used to like looking at the animal behind the fence. It was so innocent, caged, and I had always wanted to free him.

That was until he'd started chasing me.

Black and cream spotted, that dog lay dead now, its head smashed in and its brain oozing out of its scull like soup. I'd never seen real insides before that, not even on TV, and

Knight Reed hovered over it all, raging and breathy with a rock I knew now… was covered in blood. It leaked from it like a river, and Knight only dropped it when I slammed to my knees. My head falling forward, I got sick again.

At least this time I missed my shorts.

CHAPTER
ONE

Greer - age 19

The water in the sink shifted to red, deep and crimson like a vision pulled from my memories. My thoughts traveled back to the past when I'd been nine, a bleeding dog before my eyes and a boy with a dark and sinful stare looking at me. Wicked, he peered on with nothing but a pointed gleam at me.

Just like he did now.

I was aware of that same gleam hovering over me at the present, lingering as I scrubbed and scrubbed at the skin stained red. The friction of the wash burned, my skin threatening to come off as I washed it so hard. All the while that glare found me, a large presence following as the boy with the brown eyes made his way into the bathroom with me. He was no longer that boy, but a man of size and firm stature. He was a man of presence and heat that did nothing but make my heart race.

If only it could be for the right reasons.

A slow reach and Knight Reed tugged at my sleeve,

exposing skin covered in the same red I was attempting to rub away. It'd made it everywhere, even up my sleeve.

"You'll miss your arms," he said, and I found his eyes again. They immediately swallowed me up in their ebony depths, a dark sea as rigid and harsh as when we'd been kids. He'd had so much anger as a child, and that same anger stared right back at me through the mirror. Those eyes shifted, and mine did too, to me this time in the mirror. It seemed I'd missed some of that red I was attempting to wash away...

The blood coated my face like freckles.

Earlier that night

CHAPTER
TWO

Knight

Behind a drink, I saw her, remembered her.

And she still managed to get mixed up with pricks.

Greer Michaelson couldn't help getting herself in trouble, even after all this time and all these years. My frat brother Bryce's arm was around her, the king of the entitled douchebags that roamed the halls of our frat house. I didn't have to like every motherfucker here, and I especially didn't like him, a special place in hell reserved for him and his lot.

I sipped at my beer, the brother guiding Greer around. Holding her like arm candy, he didn't even acknowledge her, bumping fists with other brothers and friends. Had he actually *seen* her, he'd see her and sure as fuck wouldn't be looking away.

I fucking wasn't.

White blond hair curled a little at the ends, a pert nose and pink lips like a sweep above and below. Her chin round and her face oval, she flitted those wide eyes of hers innocently around the room. She hadn't seen me yet and may not even recognize me, a far cry from that eleven-year-old with knobby knees and hair that couldn't be tamed for shit. I also hadn't lifted a weight until junior high, and needless to say, that scrawny-ass kid had filled out in the years since. I had trouble fitting through the frames of most doors these days, height or width.

Smirking at how much Greer had changed too, I drew off my beer. Curves and supple tits she hid behind a long sleeve crop top and acid-washed jeans sitting well above her navel. The things were basically grandma cut and went well with the whole nineties MTV video thing she was trying to pull. She definitely didn't fit in this place, definitely *looked like a freshman*, and that was probably a big reason the second biggest guy in the room outside of myself preyed on her. He thought he could take advantage of that little white dove, pure and innocent as she pranced around the room with him. I hadn't seen her in over ten years, but the memories had hardly left. I mean, she fucking lived in my house, she and her mom since her mom used to clean my grandfather's manor. He basically raised me, and I saw that little dove often.

I shifted as Bryce guided Greer around, barely even speaking to her. The growl low in my throat, I recalled some of the last moments she'd been in my life. Things hadn't been pretty toward the end there, and even being eleven I'd known that. Grandfather had tried to hide a lot of things from me growing up, shelter me, but even he couldn't scrub away the real reason Greer and her mom had ultimately left. It'd been very much because of me and my grandfather's need to keep drama out of my life. I'd been very fragile back then…

Veering my attention away from Greer and the spectacle, I transferred it to another blonde who vied for my attention. Melrose pushed her slender arms around me, a model outside of her college work, but even still she couldn't reach my height. I folded an arm around her, an attempt to blend in and keep my attention off Greer fucking Michaelson. I couldn't help but be intrigued. After all, I hadn't seen her in so long and had been curious. Needless to say, a working model beneath my arm with her perfect tits pressed up against me proved to be enough to bring my head out of the past a little.

"Knight Reed. You can't say hi to your fucking bro?"

That was until the clouds opened up and douchebag rains fell in, Bryce Coventry with the blast from my past under *his* arm.

"Bryce. Bro." Ignoring Greer, I pounded the guy's fist, very much aware that eyes that sparkled like sapphire cut jewels lingered in my direction. I couldn't discover if Greer had put two and two together that she knew me yet, but she was definitely looking at me. Easing my arm back around Melrose, I tipped my chin at the girl with me. "You know Melrose."

And did Bryce know her, his eyes mischief as he smoldered and grinned at one girl while holding onto another. The guy was just a tool like that, the pair of us cut from the same cloth in a few two many ways, but that was different since one of those girls today was Greer. I knew her.

And God did she know me.

Her lips parted in the most stunning of ways, her nervous lick across them inducing all kinds of fucking images and shooting them straight into my cock. My dick strained at my fly like I'd never had a pussy before, making me uncomfortable enough to hold tight onto Melrose. She might have to take care of me a little later, and with my digits brushing against her shoulder, she definitely got the point. She put a hand on my chest. "Bryce, who's your friend?"

His friend was currently staring at me too. Like I said, she knew me. She knew our history, and the way her blue eyes bored into mine before finding Melrose told me that. She put her hand out to Melrose. "Greer Michaelson."

"Melrose Andrews." Her hand returned to my chest.

"You're new? I haven't seen you around here, the campus or anything."

"Just started actually." Greer blinked, her attention shifting *again*. Oh, yeah. She definitely knew me. Her gaze drifted back to Melrose, and when she smiled, it did appear genuine. "I'm a freshman."

"But sexy as fuck." Bryce twirled her around, and the growl rumbled deep in my chest, more unnerved than I should be. I shouldn't give a fuck about Greer Michaelson.

So why the fuck were my fingers digging into my beer bottle?

Maybe it was because I didn't want to see someone so clearly pure and innocent being gobbled up by the king of the pricks, my ring restlessly tapping my beer before bringing it up to my lips. I eased the alcohol down in a thick lump, other images clouding my vision. I'd made the mistake of coming to this girl's rescue before, something that had ultimately gotten her and her mom kicked out of my house in the first place. I remembered that thing with the dog well, my meddling well, and I brushed my fingers against Melrose's shoulder. "I know you. Don't I, Greer?"

Since I did, I might as well acknowledge it, and she appeared relieved that I had. At least, we wouldn't have to pretend anymore, and she placed a hand on her chest, nodding at me. "Right. It's been, what?"

"Ten years." And I knew them well, my smile small. "How's your mom doing?"

That's when her smile fell and shifted to something else, what? Annoyance? Disdain? Honest to God, the line traveled so thin, but I couldn't make it out. I just knew thoughts of our history were definitely playing across her mind, and whatever they entailed wasn't making her happy. "She's fine. Works on campus actually. That's why we moved back here."

And so my blast from the past had returned, her mom no doubt getting her a free education. No way could she afford the private tuition of Pembroke University, this school full of nothing but blood the pure color of blue. I was amongst that elite due to my familial ties, as most of the guys in this frat were.

The majority of us had been funneled over from my small town more than two hours away. Maywood Heights was a city of nothing but sin and the darkest elite, a brotherhood known as the Court the main reason why. Basically a boys' club, it bred our fathers and grandfathers into some of the most powerful men in this country, not just our small town, and was the reason why myself and many others in this room wore the very rings on our fingers. It had a gorilla pressed into the chrome finish, and though there may be miles between us and Maywood Heights, that didn't mean the values stayed behind. I liked to think I rose above some of the riffraff that came out of there, but even I wasn't innocent. I had a past just like everyone else, and this girl before me had seen some of it.

I nodded at Greer, what she said, and when Bryce exchanged a glance between us, I smirked at him. "Greer's mom used to work for me."

"His grandfather," she cut in, a little fire cat to that inno-cent image she portrayed. It turned me on more than I'd readily admit, her smile wide on me. "He's actually the reason she got fired."

"Fucking yeah?" Bryce balked, then slapped his hand against my chest. "What did you do?"

"Nothing worth noting now." I shifted my attention to Greer. "It's been a long time."

It had been a long time, and though I'd been a snot-nosed little kid last time I'd known her, the reaction she elicited out of me now I couldn't so easily lock down in the past and pass off as a little brat kid with an infatuation with the first girl his grandfather threw in front of him. Greer Michaelson unnerved me, was under my skin, and I felt that each time my slime ball frat brother rubbed her shoulders and pressed his nose into her white blond hair. She wasn't in his league— at all—and that was because *she* was better than *him*. Better than all this.

"How do you two know each other?" I fought heat in my voice staring at them, trying to distract myself with Melrose and her perfect tits as she pressed her pebbled nipples up against me. They strained at her top and everything, the girl hungry for me as she lazily drew fingers across my abs through my T-shirt.

Greer noticed when I glanced over to her, frowning, and though she opened her mouth to speak the douche prick wouldn't let her.

"Just met at a club tonight," he crooned, the girl basically fresh meat under his arm. He jiggled her, the ass hat basically trying to fondle her when he moved his hand around and brushed his fingers against her side boob. Greer immediately tried to ease away, clearly uncomfortable, but he kept her there.

My hand squeezed glass, and complacent, she let him hold her. He was in a position of power, and she allowed it, probably not wanting to be rude. With a tap against his arm, she did eventually push away though.

"I'm going to get a drink." A breath pulled from her lips, clear relief from no longer being fucking fondled. But with a move, Bryce got back right into that.

He brought her to him by the hips, then pinched her chin. "Get me a beer?"

She nodded, again I think to keep the peace. She passed me barely a look, and before I knew it, I was telling Melrose to follow after her.

"Get yourself something," I told her, wanting to talk to this cocksucker alone. If he was going to be talking to Greer, he wouldn't be fucking with her. I raised my bottle. "And me one too."

Melrose more than wanted to oblige like most girls in her position; being in my hometown gave me power. Then coming here, a new elite made up of people from where I was from and similar places around the globe, the same. Pembroke University had its own caste system, and as far as myself or anyone else in this fucking room was concerned, I was the king. My grandfather and my family basically funded half the programs on this campus, a building named after my family and shit. That was something I was about to let Bryce Coventry know and started right in on it the moment I asked for some of his time. It was a request mostly out of formality. The dick would do anything I fucking wanted if asked.

We ended up taking our talk upstairs and out of earshot of the party beneath. I didn't know how loud I'd get, and it would get loud if this guy fucked with me.

In his room, Bryce immediately started texting someone, and I closed the door. He had a bar set up like most of our rooms in a house meant for the privileged, so I decided to help myself to scotch.

"What's this about, brother?" he asked me, still texting when I turned around, and after I asked him about that, he smirked. "Just telling Greer where we're at. Want me to get her up here?"

Curious, I took my drink, lounging back against the wall. "Why?"

"I don't know. Thinking you, me, *her*." Waggling his eyebrows, he went back to his phone, then after, he tossed it on the bed. "I told her to go ahead and come up. We can have a good time with her. I bet she'd be game, and if she's not…" He reached over to his end table, pulling out a little bag. Clear, there were several pills inside, and it didn't take a scientist to figure out what he held.

He stalked over to me, cool as a fucking cucumber, before simulating dropping the pills into my glass of scotch.

"A little something to relax her, eh?" He nudged me, smile wide. "It'll be too easy."

Yeah, real easy, and clearly, there was no hope for this guy.

My anger only momentarily contained, I slid my glass onto the bar. "I need to talk with you."

"What about?" Back on his phone, the little fucker. His eyes danced suddenly, and with them, he pumped his fist into the air. "She's coming up, bro. Let's get a drink ready."

"Bryce?"

"What?" Like a fucking gleeful-ass kid, he quickly worked up a drink before turning down the bed. He really was going to do this, *fuck with Greer*, and I saw nothing but red, Bryce suddenly on his phone while he lounged back against sheets. He was texting with nothing if not violent delight, no doubt *texting her*, and before I thought better of it, his phone was in my hands. "Dude—"

It crashed, like literally in a million fucking pieces, when I threw it against the wall. Bryce's face shot up with red, and in an instant, his hands were on me, shoving me.

Guy had a fucking death wish.

He was immediately on the floor, one punch sending him there. I hadn't had to do much, outweighed him by at least fifty pounds, and he hit the floor like a two-ton weight.

"What. The. *Fuck*." His hand on his face, that red knob formed against his temple. It started to swell the moment he pulled his hand away, but I wasn't waiting for him to get his bearings.

I came for him, but quicker than me, he dashed onto the other side of his bed. Before I knew it, he was reaching inside his dresser drawers.

The nine millimeter was in my face.

I stopped right away, not wanting to fuck with that when I put my hands up. "Bryce, calm down."

"Calm fucking *down*?" He came around the bed, came at me while waving his gun. "Not so tough, huh?"

More like I wasn't an idiot and didn't particularly *want* to get shot. Honestly, I just needed a quick move and another punch to overpower him, but I wasn't stupid enough to take the chance. I raised my hands. "Put the gun down. We'll talk about this."

That's how I had wanted to start this, but this motherfucker was obviously crazy. I would say I hadn't meant to actually hit him. My bad on that, but he gave me no choice. He threatened Greer. *Physically* threatened Greer, and though I felt I owed her nothing, it wouldn't be on me that she got hurt. I'd done that to her before.

I just didn't want to do it again.

I had a conscience, and that was what this all was, nothing more. Bryce Coventry was a new breed of asshole, even for me and all my sins in the past.

His hand gripped around that gun like a vise, his arm shaking. "What's this about?"

I didn't have much to talk him down with, this guy completely unhinged. I mean, he pulled a fucking gun on me after only getting hit, so I knew trying to talk to him rationally at all when it came to Greer might be ill done. If anything, he might get closer to her just because he knew that was what this was about.

"I found out about some things," I said, reaching for something else, and his eyes narrowed.

"What kind of things?"

"Things about you." I lowered my hands, but still let him see them. I tipped my chin. "I heard about that stripper, bro."

"Stripper?"

I nodded. "I heard about her and what you did to her." The act was merely amongst the list of dark deeds that went on in his house, but this fucker? He took the cake. He not only raped her from what I heard but bragged about it to more than one guy around here, guys he clearly trusted but who didn't have his confidence. I raised my hands. "Now lower the gun or others are going to know about it. People you don't want to know."

"Well, maybe I should just blow your fucking head off." He honed the gun in on my head, that fucking stupid. "Maybe I should just pull the trigger now."

"You do that and someone will find the pictures." A bluff, nothing more, but he didn't know that. I lifted my chin. "Pictures of what you've done will be everywhere. I'll make it happen, and you know I will. Pulling that trigger won't stop it."

He should fear me, fear who I was, because even in death, I had capabilities. That was something he and all the other guys around here knew. We all came from powerful families, this guy no exception. Even still, he didn't have a lick on my life, new money from the south as far as I knew. He walked up on this campus like he owned the place, had with his big dick complex since freshman year. It was like he was trying to *prove* he was one of us, but what he was doing now showed me he wasn't. Had it been me, I already would have shot the fucker to get him out of my face. Not lethal, but yeah, I would have shot his ass. If anything, to prove something, who I was.

"And they'll find out about the other pictures," I threatened, bluffing more. "All the other things you've done." A God complex, this one, but even still, me lowering my hands and coming straight toward him had Bryce backing off, backing way. He moved with every stride I took. I smiled. "You know all the other things you've done."

And he did, whatever he was coming up with in his head making him back away more. A fear in his eyes elicited by nothing but threats from me. I'd heard about a lot of the shit Bryce had gotten into, but outside of the stripper, there wasn't enough to ruin. Clearly, he was finding something else, though, something in his eyes that brought a true terror within them.

He backed up against the door, shaking his head. "You

wouldn't. I…" Eyes wild, he shook the gun, his complete body fucking quivering. "I didn't do nothing with that girl, and I don't care what she says."

Hesitating, I stayed back, honest to shit unaware of what he was referring to, but that didn't seem to matter.

Bryce had the gun in a different place now, tapping the handle against his head like he was having a break down. He lowered to his knees. "I didn't know she was in fucking junior high, bro. I swear I didn't."

What the fuck?

"She only told me after. I swear, but she was fucking willing!"

Disgusted, I approached, and he stood, that gun back on me. I lifted my hands again. "Bryce—"

"No. Fuck!" He brought the gun up to his temple, shaking again and my eyes grew wide.

"Bryce."

"No, Knight. No!" A blubbering mess, tears shot down from his eyes. "You know the pressure. You know who we are to this place, and I can't, I…" He stabilized the gun against his head. "I can't go down for that."

His finger moved around the trigger, and outside of everything else, even when I had that gun pointed toward my face, I hadn't been experiencing the terror that froze me now. It was because I knew what he was about to do…

And what the would mean for me after.

Greer

Knight Reed…

Holy fucking shit.

The beer bottles shook in my hands as I made my way upstairs. Bryce said he headed up to his room to get something real quick and I could give him his there, my brain spinning at the course of events. I hadn't seen or heard from Knight in *at least* ten goddamn years, not since he'd gone crazy, killed a dog, and basically gotten my mom and me kicked out his house.

Wild.

He'd really gone fucking crazy. Had to have since he'd *killed a dog*. I mean, what kind of eleven-year-old boy did that? *And* had the nerve to look triumphant about it. The whole thing had been sick, and needless to say, it'd scared the crap out of me. I'd told my mom who'd told his grandpa, and though I'd been pretty young at the time, his grandfather's annoyance at the whole thing had been pure fact. Next thing I knew, my mom and I had been asked to leave Knight's house, my mom jobless, and later, the two of us homeless. We'd literally lived in my mom's car until I hit middle school, searching for steady work and a safe place to live that long. There had been no hope in Maywood Heights, not after Knight's grandpa had gotten through with us. Again, I'd been young, but from what I understood, I'd been a witness to scandal and his grandfather hadn't wanted any of that for his grandkid.

The golden boy with a chip on his shoulder.

God fuck, had he been smug now, asking all nonchalantly how my mom was like *he* hadn't put us both out on our asses so many years ago. My only annoyance was that he'd been fucking hot, large with these big hands that could just...

Shaking all the shit out, I basically gave a little war cry. I could handle Knight Reed. I might not have been able to then, being young, but I could now. In any sense, I clearly was hanging with his friend Bryce tonight so maybe I wouldn't have to see him anymore.

I forced out the images of a strong back and huge arms that could probably take no effort at all to rail me freaking good. I didn't have a whole lot of experience with that considering I was a virgin, but my dildo, Mr. Sprinkles, definitely did the job any college guy could do.

At least that was what I convinced myself.

Blowing air through my lips, I forced the thoughts of *Knight* out of my mind and headed to the second door on the left. Bryce's text said that was his room. Lifting the bottles, I started to knock, but heard voices, Bryce's and someone else's. Muffled, I couldn't really hear anything, and they might not have heard me knock anyway. After all, they were talking.

Instead, I decided to invite myself in and almost dropped the bottles on the floor the moment I made contact with Knight Reed's eyes. He was in there, in there with Bryce, and the instant I waltzed through the door, his dark gaze slipped over to me. I had no idea what to make of that until my own gaze shifted over to Bryce. He said something, something about not being able to go down for something.

A pop, just one, and reality as I knew it shifted before me. The beer bottles dropped from my hands as I jumped, something wet hitting my face, and when I opened my eyes, my arms were covered in red. My white, long-sleeve shirt had spots, my hands dotted the same, and when I gazed down, I saw Bryce amongst shattered glass and wasted booze, a flow of blood pooling the floor around his head. He had a gun in his hand, a freaking gun.

"Greer…"

My gaze shot over to Knight Reed, eyes the color of a young buck's coat twitched wide with absolute horror. The expression on his face matched, my body and limbs covered in blood like something out of Carrie.

I fell, so slow and like nothing in the movies. It was like I was outside of myself watching me fall, peering on as Knight called my name again. Things went so, so hazy.

But then they gratefully went dark.

CHAPTER
THREE

Knight

I caught her before she hit the ground.

Shit. Shit. Fuck.

Honest to shit I hadn't expected Bryce to actually off himself. I'd just wanted to scare him a bit, threaten him with the truth…

But not this.

Greer's weight felt nothing but light in my arms. Most barbells I lifted were three times heavier than that. I tapped her face with my fingers. "Greer?"

She'd seen *everything*, but gratefully wasn't seeing anything now. A Coventry with a hole blasted into his head, but at least that was the side he'd fallen on.

My grandpa is going to freaking kill me.

The man wasn't one for drama and this whole situation would definitely do that for him. I obviously had to call him after this, bring in the heavy artillery to get me the fuck out of this, but at the present, all I was seeing was a flush face, a girl with her eyes closed and covered in blood. She looked awful, and this was my fault.

What do I do? What do I do?

My first thought was to run with her, get her out of this situation. If she wasn't here, she didn't see anything and the fact that no one was rushing up here now let me know the party downstairs was at least doing something. That base I could feel in my chest, our frat house in the middle of bumfuck nowhere. We had a bit of a cabin setting over here, out in the nature and the woods for hiking and shit. There was a lot of money that came through here, therefore we got the privacy we wanted.

And thank fuck for that now.

I gave it no more thought before picking Greer up and hooking her arms around my neck. I was going to get her out here, no witnesses but Bryce and me. The fact of the matter was she was a loose end my grandfather definitely didn't need to know about that.

"Greer? I need you to wake up for me, baby." Where the "baby" came from I didn't fucking know, my finger curled against her jaw. She moaned, but didn't do anything more than that, and without thought, I cursed before holding her and wiping away any evidence she or I had been in the room. Obviously, the beer bottles were there, but for all the police would know, Bryce was just attempting to get piss ass drunk before killing himself.

At least that's what Grandfather would most likely convince them of.

I'd be calling him as soon as I got Greer out of here, and after taking my scotch and the glass, I headed out the back way through the room. All our rooms led to balconies and then outside, something I took advantage of right away. The garages were out back there too, and after finding my ride, a dark Escalade, I shoved Greer inside.

She moaned again, lolling her little head, but gratefully

didn't wake up. I didn't need her fighting me. I was trying to get her out of here. I strapped in, opened the garage, then zoomed the fuck out of there. I put the cabin in my rearview mirror as I headed off in the direction of campus. I didn't know where I was going, but at the present, any place was better than where we were.

I ended up pulling into a motel lot only minutes later, and after jerking a hoodie out the back and slipping it on, I went to check in. I hadn't gotten any blood on me until I picked up Greer so I had to at least hide that with the hoodie. The guy inside hadn't asked too many questions, and after I got the room key, I went back to my Escalade. I drove Greer and me toward the back of the lot, the guy at the desk giving me a room far away as requested. We pulled up there, and I shut off my car.

"Greer?" Another touch to her cheek, a soft one to wake her up. Her white lashes fluttered, nothing more, and I knew waking her up wasn't happening, at least not right now.

Shooting a curse, I hopped outside, coming around for her. I opened the door, and her tiny body basically fell out into my arms again. I might think about that more, the way she smelled like frickin' candy, had I not been trying to get her out of public view.

Between her and the keys, I did manage to get the door open, another mumbled moan against the shell of my ear, as I got her into the room. A double queen, I let Greer lay on one. She curled up into herself, still fucking out of it and she was covered in so much blood it'd been ridiculous. She looked like she'd killed Bryce herself.

Since at the present we both appeared to be in the clear now, I took out my phone to call my grandpa. He'd need to do some damage control for me. I mean, I'd been into some fucked up shit but never had I had a dead body on my hands. That was even a new one for me.

My finger hovered over his name before a groan to my

right darted my gaze in that that direction. Greer had her hand on her head, but the moment she looked at her fingers, she shook. Her mouth parted, a scream clearly on her lips, and I rushed over to her.

"Greer?"

A jump and she was scurrying across the bed, true and utter terror in her eyes like one of those final days she'd last seen me. It was literally the same look she'd given me after I'd killed Old Man Peabody's dog, like she was scared of me.

She should be.

I'd had no regrets that day like I didn't now; no, not for trying to get her out of my frat. She would have been worse off left behind, and at the mercy of my grandfather, worse like she would have been had that dog been allowed to live. I'd saved her from that like I did now.

But try convincing her of that.

"Knight? What the fuck?"

I edged closer, and she moved back on the bed, another step and she was off it. She ran like a fucking prized pony out the gate, and though I had size, I had sped too. I grabbed her by her little wrist and jerked her back so hard she did scream.

Snapping a hand across her mouth, I gathered her up by her hips, the girl biting at me. She got a mouth full of my Court ring, my flesh next but I didn't even flinch. I tossed her on the bed, and she scurried again, but this time, I'd been prepared. I lunged at her, pulling her immediately beneath me.

"What are you doing!"

My hand covered her mouth again, a muted scream behind. She jabbed at me with her knees, but using my weight, I pinned her down. She bit me again, and unexpected, I cursed this time, slamming her head against the pillow to stop fighting me.

"Shut the fuck up," I growled, and almost instantly, she froze beneath me, a harsh fear she should probably have. I outweighed her by a lot, and she wouldn't leave this room unless I saw fit.

Trembling now, good. My priority was keeping her safe, and if I hurt her in the process, so be it. I honed in. "You'll stay quiet. *Silent*, you hear me?"

She did, her nod incessant, but even still I gave her an incentive. My hand formed around her delicate throat, the jump beneath my hand.

"You scream and I squeeze," I warned. "You understand?"

Again, a nod and another swallow. My thumb dragged along her throat, and she shivered, gripping my arms. She could probably scratch me this way but was smart enough not to.

Letting go of her mouth, I got one of her hands, letting her know not to try anything when I shifted more of my body weight on her. My cock surged between us, something I was sure she definitely felt. I couldn't help it with all her delightful heat beneath me, that softness between her thighs.

I shifted a knee between them, brushing her mound, and she pulled in a breath. Her chin tipped up. "What are you doing?"

I honestly didn't know, starting this all just to keep her quiet. Putting knees on either side of her body, I hovered over her. "You're going to listen to me. Listen to what I have to say. What you saw tonight could cause problems for you."

"What kind of problems?"

Too much fucking talk. My hand squeezed her throat, another incentive, and it worked. She stiffened immediately, her face scrunched in fear. I didn't want to scare her. Honestly didn't, but if it kept her quiet…

I pressed a finger to her lips. "I'm going to let you go so you can wash up. And after, we'll talk more about this."

I had no idea how much we'd actually talk about, what I'd give her, but it'd be enough to keep her quiet. I didn't need her asking any more questions, giving me more of that lip and mouth. It really could get her hurt. I knew the people I came from well.

I'd do the same to protect my grandfather, rid the world of any loose ends if I had to for him. He was pretty much all I had in the world, at least in every way that mattered.

Though Greer said nothing, I did let her off the bed. She lay there like a scared little animal, shrunk to size, and really, a little dove. I jerked my chin toward the bathroom. "Wash up."

She didn't need any more incentive and when she got up, I gave her a warning, a look not to test me and run. I'd get her again.

I think she saw that in my eyes.

Little footfalls and she was easing into the bathroom, starting to close the door but I came over and stopped her for a second.

I peered around, making sure there were no windows for her to try and do something foolish. "Get to it."

The water ran as I eased the door shut, but not completely closed. She didn't need that much privacy, but she would need a change of clothes. Thinking about the only person I knew close by who'd have some, I dialed my friend Royal. He recently started at Pembroke, working before so he came in as freshmen. His fiancée December was a recent transfer student, a junior like me, and they'd gotten engaged at the beginning of term.

"Bro, you do know what fucking time it is?" Sleep in his voice, he huffed. "The fuck you want?"

Mary Sunshine and how responsible to be going to bed before midnight. That'd have been his girl December's doing, no doubt. I smirked. "I need a favor."

"What kind?"

"A big one. December with you?"

"Yeah, why?"

"I need to borrow some of her clothes." They'd hang on

Greer a little since she was smaller, more petite and didn't have December's height but they'd do.

Silence for a second. "The fuck? You going to wear them or something?"

I rolled my eyes. "No, asshole. I need them for a friend, hers got ruined."

Water slowed in the distance, still running but definitely not at full power. Perhaps, Greer was getting done in there.

"Do I want to know?" Royal asked in my ear, but it sounded like he was getting up.

"Just bring them." I ended the call before heading toward the bathroom. If the water slowed, Greer just might be done.

Looks like it might be time to talk.

THE PRESENT

Greer

I'd turned down the water to hear what was going on outside the door, voices on the other side. It'd sounded like Knight was speaking to someone, but the moment he ended his call, I blasted that water right back up, scrubbing my hands and the water painting in red. Currently, Knight stood behind me, watching me while I scrubbed.

Until, well, he didn't.

His touch on me had caused me to tremble, his fingers tugging up my sleeves. But the moment he made eye contact with me through the bathroom mirror, I found I couldn't keep it. My face was coated in fucking blood, and I felt myself grow faint again, woozy. I'd never been good with blood, but with Knight behind me, I forced myself to nut the hell up and bring water to my face. He'd *yelled* at me tonight, tackled me and kidnapped me.

What the fuck?

I scrubbed at the spots in quick time, my hair also dotted in bright crimson splatter. Noticing my labor, Knight cursed and backed up off me. I'd been able to breathe for only a little bit before he started to work his shirt off.

A naked torso with perfectly chiseled abs pooled heat between my legs, a reminder of *him* between my legs. He'd touched me with his knee, the brunt of his hard weight pinning me to the bed. It'd gotten me excited in confusing ways, fear that he'd been pinning me down but also excitement because he'd touched me. The whole thing was as hella fucking confusing as watching him and his nakedness, the big guy sauntering his way over to me and dabbing his T-shirt on my face. He wet it, then dabbed again, and I flinched when he brushed it near my lips.

He frowned. "Relax. I won't hurt you."

Unless I gave him a reason, right? I talked? I folded my arms. "Can I speak?"

A sigh passed his lips, and when he shook his head, he dabbed my face again. "Depends on what you'll say."

That arrogant fuck. I wanted to scream at him, lunge and kick my feet, but something told me he'd have me out of this room and right on my back again. Something told me he'd make me *burn*, and as much as that confused me, I definitely hadn't wanted that.

Instead, I decided to remain silent, allowing him to touch my face and chest with his damp shirt while trying not to reveal I felt anything about it. I tried to mask my fear, but each brush of my skin with rough fingertips worked a deep chill through me. My throat jumped when he touched it, and cursing again, he stepped back.

"You're going to need a shower," he concluded, and my stomach instantly turned. Would he *make* me shower? Force himself on me like he had before? I'd been confused, but not enough to want that. He threw fingers through brown-black hair. "I got a buddy bringing you clothes."

"A buddy?"

He nodded before tossing his shirt in the sink. He ran the faucet, drenching it before wringing it out and hanging it off the towel rack. "His fiancee is a little taller than you, but it should work."

Why was he helping me? Why were we *here* and not back at the frat house? Bryce had killed himself. We needed to call the fucking cops, not flee the scene. I closed my eyes, forcing a shuddered breath. "Can I speak?"

"You didn't the first time."

"Well, I want to now," I snipped, my eyes flashing at the dark haze that cast over Knight's normally brown eyes. They went brown-black, just like his hair, and taking a boot, he propped it back against the closed door.

"Shoot," he said, irony in what he said, but I had a feeling there wouldn't be any candidness here. Not if he didn't want it. He was definitely in charge here, and because he was, I forced myself to check how I actually wanted to act.

"I don't understand why we're here."

Apparently an easy one for him, he smirked. He put a hand out. "You're obviously a little messy. Here to clean yourself up?"

That wasn't what I meant and he knew that. My nostrils flared. "I mean, why are we here and not back at the frat? Why aren't we calling the cops?"

"The situation is being handled." Too cool like he normally dealt with dead bodies every day. Maybe he did, so relaxed about it.

And then there'd been that dog.

He'd been cool then too, almost angry at eleven years old with a damn bloodied rock in his hand. Knight Reed was obviously into some crazy fucking shit, a screw or two loose himself. Since I didn't know what I was dealing with here, I tabled my temper, forcing myself to calm down. "It's being handled?"

"Yes."

"You do know Bryce killed himself."

"Yes, *obviously*." His fingers worked a chrome ring, his thumb flicking at it with some kind of animal mouth on the finish. "Like I said, it's being handled."

"By whom? Knight, shouldn't we call the cops—"

His thumb left the ring, and his hand covered my mouth, gripping it like he had on the bed. He tasted like blood, metallic and heat. The warmth, that fire had obviously been him and the rest someone else.

I choked down sickness as his fingers dug into my cheeks, his eyes terribly cold.

"The cops will be called when it's time," he said, dark gaze roving over my face. "But that's something you won't have to deal with. That's why you're here. You're here so you don't have to deal with it."

But deal with what? A suicide? What could I possibly have to deal with? The cops would only just question me, none it my or his fault.

But maybe something different was going on here, something I obviously didn't understand. A knock hit and Knight turned, gazing through the room and to the other door. He pressed a finger to his mouth. "You say nothing."

Understanding, I stood there and frozen, I didn't think I could do anything anyway. I was locked where I stood, Knight's back muscles roving under tanned skin as he made his way to the door. He opened it, and another guy stood there with a duffel bag, and though there was some distance between us, he was basically just as hot as Knight was. Blond, he took one look at Knight and sneered.

"Why the hell are you half naked?" he asked, then his brow jumped. "And is that blood—"

Knight shushed him before they both ended up outside the room, the door snapping shut behind them. Breathing, I instantly left the bathroom, thinking maybe there might be a way out. I came up with nothing but the front window, and since Knight was obviously behind that, I cursed.

I ended up peeking outside the blinds, Knight and the other hot guy a ways away from the door. They stood in front of an emerald-green ride, expensive looking and no doubt suped up. I didn't know much about cars but the thing looked like something straight out of Fast and the Furious.

Honing in, I watched Knight and the guy, the blond just as familiar to me as Knight had been tonight. It'd obviously had been awhile, but I'd seen him before too, recognized his hair and bone structure.

I sucked in a breath at the recalled thought, the guy Knight's friend, Royal. He used to hang out at Knight's house all the time; when I saw him, Royal always with him. Knight often hung out with several boys, Jax and LJ the other two I recalled. There was a girl too back then. Paige, I thought her name was?

I gripped the curtains. Only one boy in particular had been with Knight that day he'd gone crazy, killed that dog. *Royal* had been the one holding it down and letting him do it. Did they both have plans for me tonight? Something as equally dark? Touching my throat, I watched as Royal smacked at Knight's chest. Clearly annoyed with him about something, he raised and dropped his hands, and when he shoved at Knight again, I thought the guy had a death wish. Knight was like two of him.

For whatever reason, Knight took it, and though he too looked annoyed, he did bump Royal's fist after he handed him the bag. I heard him mention something about thanks before Royal left and got into the running car. At that point, the front window went down but it wasn't Royal to do it.

A girl sat in the front seat, one with dark hair and ridiculously pretty. She looked like an Instagram model, and after looking over at Royal, speaking to him for a second, she turned and frowned at Knight. I saw her mouth, "Really?" before shaking her head.

He did the same at her, but before anything else could be done I saw Knight stride back toward the door.

I let go of the blinds immediately, scurrying back to the bathroom. I stood there stiffly like I hadn't moved, and Knight rolled his eyes, the moment he made eye contact with me.

"Enjoy the show?" he asked, angling his big body into the bathroom. Reaching into the bag, he pulled out a tank and a pair of shorts, pointing at me. "You're breathing like you just ran a mile."

Christ.

I said nothing, letting him hand off the clothes to me. They were only a size or two too big, not bad. They were obviously that girl's, Royal's fiancee, Knight said.

"Was that Royal Prinze?" I asked, since I'd been caught. I shrugged. "It looked like him."

Knight's jaw moved a little before he propped the bag on his shoulder. "It was. Any more questions?"

Only like a million, but I kept them silent for now. My lips worked, but when Knight left the bathroom, I didn't do anything. He faced me, frowning again. "Need help taking off your clothes?"

Because I didn't, I closed the bathroom door, and before he could make good on the threat, I started the water in the shower. Pressing my ear to the door, I heard a distinct and deep chuckle on the other side, and I growled at how arrogant this guy was. He clearly thought he could do anything he wanted.

Not knowing what else to do, I quickly pulled open the shower, and after stripping off my clothes, I eased myself inside the heat. I think that was where it all hit me, what had happened tonight, what was still happening. The red fell from my hair and flesh like eerie paint, and I pressed my head to the shower tiles.

What the fuck is going on?

Terrified, I shivered, holding myself. I had no idea what Knight planned for tonight, and I didn't even have my things, my purse and stuff. If I had to wager, I'd guess he took them from me. Maybe in the car he obviously got us here in? I didn't know. I just knew I made that shower last, and by the time I got out, I couldn't breathe and not just from the heat.

The door had been cracked when I opened the shower, a reminder that he was there and obviously needed control. I didn't know if he'd watched me or just wanted me to know what was going on here, his heavy hand on all things Greer.

I slipped the shorts on, then the top. My bra and underwear were black so at least, none of the blood could been seen on that. Not so much for my jeans and shirt, and I bunched them up, coming out of the bathroom. Knight sat on one of the beds when I came out, his thumb carelessly swiping over his phone. He was also in a new change of clothes, shorts and a hoodie with the sleeves ripped off them. They displayed the sight of biceps the size of most men's thighs, his dark hair wet and obviously freshly washed.

"You showered?" I asked, quiet as I came completely out the bathroom. His head jerked up, but then, he shrugged, reaching his hand out for the clothes in my hands.

"Got an adjoining room," he said, balling up my stuff and forcing it into the bag Royal had brought him. He stood. "I always keep clothes in the car for the gym."

And that's definitely what he looked ready for, muscled calves and thick legs. Wetting my lips, I panned away, taking a seat on the bed. I could have cursed myself for not checking to see if he'd gotten another room. There was a door there, and I hadn't thought to look.

All of that pointless now, I settled on the bed. Knight dropped the bag at the door, then came back over to me. He took a seat on the opposite bed, and I froze as he reached a hand out and tugged me over to him.

"What are you doing?"

He eased me down next to him, smelling like cologne and peppermint. He chewed gum, his hard heat next to me when his shoulder touched my arm. "About to explain to you what's about to happen here."

Quiet, my mouth dried, his fingers coming to brush my chin. A pinch and he had me looking right at him, his eyes just as hard and cold as they'd been before. I swallowed. "What's about to happen here?"

I watched, brave when I forced away any kind of fear to be visibly shone on me face, his thumb moving and encircling my mouth before bringing my ear to his lips. "You're going to be a good, little dove. That's what's about to happen."

My chest jumped. "Little dove?"

His fingers flicked my white blond hair, tugging at it. "A sweet, little innocent dove that does exactly what she's told."

"Which is?" I played his game but mostly out of fear, trying so hard not to tremble in his hands. I didn't want to show him weakness, that I truly was terrified of him as much as that final day in the woods, a boy over a dead dog with a bloody rock in his hands.

Knight tugged my lips apart. He made me pout when he suddenly gripped my jaw and jerked my head up to look at him. His eyes narrowed. "You're not fooling anyone, you know? I see what you're doing. All those thoughts moving around in your head." His fingers folded into my hair, gripping that next. He tugged at the root. "But if you know what's good for you, you'll shut that shit down. You're to forget what happened at the frat tonight. You're to *deny* you were ever even there. As far as the world is concerned, Bryce Coventry blew his fucking brains out, and you were back on campus wherever the fuck you were, doing whatever the fuck you freshman do."

I gasped, his grip in my hair hurting. "Why?"

"You don't ask why." He pointed a finger. "You just do what you're told. You do that because you're a good little dove who answers to me."

Forcing the lump down my throat, tears burned my eyes. "I don't understand."

"And you won't. Maybe not ever. Just know that after I leave you tonight, we weren't together. You didn't see me and you weren't at my frat house."

He was… letting me go? I trembled. "You're not going to hurt me?"

He let go right away, getting up from the bed, and I nearly passed out when his weight left up. He grabbed the bag at the door, then after, grabbed me. "I won't do anything unless I have to. I won't do anything until you *stop* being a good little dove."

Shaking, I nodded. His hand left, but I stayed there, holding my arms.

"You coming? Or am I going to have to carry you out?"

Not willing to give him a reason to, I quickly gathered my bearings. He wiped down the room, then I followed him out. Eventually, I trailed him over to a dark Escalade, and I realized that was how we'd gotten here tonight. I had been passed out.

The lights flashed when Knight unlocked it, and when I got inside, I found my purse right away. He'd left it there, and it had actually managed not to get slathered in Bryce's blood.

I checked the thing as Knight got behind the wheel, well aware of his eyes on me as he started the car. I had just a couple text messages from my roommates. I had three, but nothing dire. They just wanted to know how things went with Bryce and me tonight. We'd all been at the club earlier when I met him.

Me: Good. On my way home.

Haley: Did you fuck him?

Keisha: Oh, my God you can't ask if she fucked him… did you?

Sophie: Yeah, tell us.

I hadn't… fucked him and the night couldn't have gone worse.

Knight noticed my thumbs hovered over my text message, his eyes darkening before returning to the road. "Friends of yours?"

"Roommates."

He nodded. "Well, I hope you told them you had a good time whatever the fuck you were doing tonight."

My throat closing up, that's exactly what I did, shoving my phone back in my purse right away. Knight ran his hand over his steering wheel, that ring on his finger glistening before he stared my way. "Where do you live? That's where you're going next."

A command, not a request and one I didn't disagree with.

I told him Thurston Hall, silent the rest of the drive. I wasn't really very talkative after being shoved on a bed, then forced to shower a guy's blood off my body, but I had a feeling Knight rather enjoyed that. He actually turned on music, heavy rock, and threw his beefy arm out the window. He alternated between that and hip hop, his tastes diverse and varied. We pulled up to Thurston Hall in the back, which was okay because I had a key to the back entry, all residents did. This was a freshman only hall so it was pretty quiet tonight, most people in bed before Monday's classes. Knight turned off the car, and I didn't move right away, fearing a change in the air might goad the madman inside. He stayed silent, running that ring across his steering wheel again.

"Promise tonight won't be a problem for you," he said, and for the first time, I heard something in his voice. It wasn't as hard, as he swung his dark eyes on me. He frowned. "Because if it will be that's something I need to know now."

I was to say nothing about what happened tonight. I was to keep quiet, a certainty obviously needed from him.

"Promise what will be a problem?" I asked, and it was obviously the right answer. Not only did Knight face the road again, he unlocked the door.

I opened, basically falling out, his ride was so high. I closed the door, and he didn't even watch before peeling away from the street. I headed up to the entry doors, but hadn't even opened them before my phone buzzed.

The text message floated across my screen.

Unknown: Remember to be a good little dove.

This man had my phone number, had probably gotten it when I'd been showering. This man had his shadow over life…

And this man wanted me to know it.

CHAPTER
FOUR

Knight

My grandpa was already at the frat house by the time Royal and I pulled up to it. And how did I know? Because the whole house was quiet. Seriously, there was only one fucking squad car there in the street, the officer tipping his hat at Royal and me before getting back into his car. Grandfather had taken care of everything, clearly.

Royal tapped a hand against my chest, and we headed inside, my buddy coming along with me for this second ride of the night. I hadn't needed him, but after explaining everything to him at the motel, he'd said he wanted to come along. He'd wanted to drop December off at her apartment first, and since I'd had Greer, we met up after we had clear cars. December had fought him, but gratefully Greer hadn't fought me. The little dove knew her place in all this, but I'd definitely be following up with her and keeping her mouth quiet.

Especially since Gramps looked pissed.

He chatted with a few of the frat brothers. Though not many. Serious to shit, there was like nobody here, the party

completely ended and nothing but the usuals moseying
about. One would think a dead body hadn't been upstairs
tonight, and upon seeing Royal and me, Grandfather touched
the shoulder of one of my fraternity brothers. He knew the
guy well, also Court with the gorilla ring on his finger. Back
home, we called it the King, the mascot of my high school,
but it meant a hell of a lot more than that. That gorilla's bite
meant power, influence, and something I clearly had here.

"I'm sorry for the loss of your fraternity brother, son,"
Grandfather said, frowning. "I know it's been an eventful
night, but do try to get some sleep. I've taken care of everything, and you don't have to worry."

My frat brother shook his head. "I just had no idea Bryce
was so troubled. Fucking crazy." The guy's head sagged
before shaking Grandfather's hand. "Thank you for being
here, Mr. Reed, *and* taking care of all this."

"Of course, and say hello to your father for me."

Nothing more than that before my frat bother passed me,
pounding both Royal's fist and mine before leaving the room.
Like I said, we all knew each other well being from the same
town, and obviously, Grandfather really had taken care of
everything. I'd called him after I'd dropped off Greer,
explained everything to him, and he'd told me to meet up
with him at the house after I'd gotten done with Royal. I'd
used my buddy as an alibi tonight, saying after Bryce shot
himself in front of me, I'd headed over to his place to change.
Royal wasn't a part of the fraternity, and frankly, he'd had
enough of any type of brotherhood after we left Maywood
Heights. I honest to God hadn't blamed him. Because of that
town and the corruption, his own dad was in prison. A long
story but it was true. Royal lost a lot growing up in Maywood
Heights. We all had.

A thought for another day, I headed over to my grandpa.

"Grandfather," I said, the man touching my shoulder as he
hugged me. He played it off that he wasn't pissed to fucking

hell about having to come here in the middle of the night and cover up a suicide, but even in his navy evening jacket, he was simmering. I knew because this man, for all intents and purposes, was my dad. I'd lost my own father early, my mom basically not close behind, and Grandfather had been there to pick up the pieces. His expression was stern when he pulled away.

"A Coventry? Really, boy?" he said to me, but did nod at Royal when he pulled away. Grandfather braced Royal's hand. "I take it you haven't been able to keep my grandson out of trouble with your arrival this term?"

Royal liked my grandpa. We all did. He seemed like the one sane one out of all Court fathers and grandfathers despite being so stern. With a short but genuine smile, Grandfather pulled Royal in as well, his hug firm.

"When have I ever been able to control him?" Royal stated, and truth, I said nothing beside him. I did what the fuck I wanted to do, *end of story*, but I hadn't wanted this tonight. Royal frowned. "The first I'd heard of what happened was shortly before you."

"Mmm." Grandfather tapped a cane, only partially needing it. The other was just to intimidate on the days his arthritis wasn't bothering him at all. A hand and he led Royal and me through my own house, our destination the lower balcony out back to talk candidly. No one was really around, and though I wasn't surprised, still my grandpa's capabilities astounded me.

"I take it everything has been handled?" I asked, leaning against the wooden railing. Scenic, the frat house looked over a valley of trees and wilderness, a winding hill on the way down to Pembroke U's campus. The quad could actually be seen a little bit from here, at least the steeple of the administration building.

Grandfather eased himself into a lounge chair, and barely a minute out there, another one of my frat brother's joined us.

He had a cup of something hot in his hand, steaming in the night, and he handed it off to my grandpa, basically fucking bowing after.

"Good to see you, Mr. Reed," he said. "And thank you again for tonight. Keeping all this quiet? My father would have handed it to me if I'd had to call him."

I was sure of a lot of them would, none of our dads, uncles, or grandpas down for scandal.

Another previous Court member, my brother bumped a fist against mine, Royal's second, before excusing himself.

"I take it that answers your question?" Grandfather stirred what was no doubt black tea, his favorite. His sip slow, he stared out into the abyss of trees and stars, something he most likely did around my age as well. This college and this frat were legacy, the ivy league closest to our hometown. A lot of power ebbed and flowed from within these four walls. Grandfather's lips pursed tight. "Though not without a significant amount of labor on my part. I owe the county police department new uniforms and gear for all their officers." He frowned. "Then there's the Coventry boy's family."

Both Royal and I cringed. My shoulder lifted. "Will it be an issue or…"

"Of course not." His spoon stopped in his tea. "The boy's father is a close business partner of mine and any thoughts of an attempt at retribution was easily swayed with a few calls and nice settlement in the man's favor. He also gets to keep all his businesses so, of course, he was very reasonable about it."

Of course. Gotta love blackmail.

Grandfather sighed. "But none of this *should have been* an issue. What happened tonight shouldn't have happened, and *I* shouldn't have had to be here to clean it up."

"How was I supposed to know the guy was crazy? That he'd kill himself?" I scrubbed my hand through my hair. "We were just talking, and shit escalated."

Bryce Coventry offed himself in the end because of pure

guilt, only. Sure, it'd been guilt I'd accidentally gotten him to admit to but that hadn't been on me. I'd just wanted him to stay his sick ass away from Greer. When it came to looking just at those facts, I'd been in the right and had no regrets. Bryce Coventry's blood was on his own hands, and as far as I was concerned, I was good.

Grandfather's lips worked after taking a sip. "And that's all? A heated discussion and self-admittance? At least, that's what you told me. That he admitted to something… disturbing, and when he thought you knew, well, you know happened next."

As far as what my grandpa needed to know to clean this up, then put the matter to bed? Yes, that was all that went down. "That's all."

Grandfather leaned back. His lips pursed again. "And it was just you two boys upstairs in the room? I have to say, Knight. It wasn't easy getting people out of here, making sure no one actually saw anything. *Knew* about anything but the need to know in our circle." Grandfather tsked below his mustache. "Gratefully, it seems to have only been you and the Coventry boy to actually be privy to what went on in that room. No one even heard the gunshot."

That was what I figured since no one came. I eased hands inside my pockets.

"So there's no one else I need to worry about?" he asked me again, straightforward. "Because I really don't want to have to come down here and clean up more mess."

I felt Royal's gaze on me, well in the know that someone else was around. I told my buddy everything, but not only did he stay quiet, I did too. I shook my head. "No, sir. No one else."

Grandfather faced Royal as if needing confirmation. He knew that I told him everything, and when Royal said nothing, my grandpa went back to his tea. Royal and I stayed there, silent as we watched one of the oldest members of

Court enjoy his tea. As far as my grandpa was concerned, no one else beside Bryce and me were in that bedroom tonight. Because the alternative would be very, *very* bad. My grandpa didn't just cover something up when he wanted something gone, he erased it.

Greer and her mom had been lucky to escape the first time.

A FEW DAYS LATER

CHAPTER
FIVE

Greer

A nervous fucking wreck, my new MO when one of my roommates, Haley, popped her head into my bedroom. I literally jumped a foot full off the bed, sleeping when I heard the door open. I pulled the sheets down, and Hales was pouting.

"You all right, boo?" she asked, folding herself in. "You haven't left this room like all week. The girls and I are starting to worry? Thinking about calling your mom?"

God fuck would that be a bad idea, *even worse* if my mom roped in my stepdad Ben. He was a cop, campus police actually.

I scrubbed into my hair, my demeanor cool, calm, and collected when I raised my legs under the sheets. At least, I tried to appear that way. I forced a grin. "I'm good. Just been stressed."

"Stressed?"

Yeah, the epitome of, but since my experience the other night with a devil heir who was basically sex on legs was on the need to know, I forced my grin again. "I'm good. Don't worry. Like I said, just stress. This whole college thing is new."

Hales definitely got that. Premed, her coursework was insane and our other roommates, Keisha and Sophie weren't much better off. They were pre-law if one could believe that, making me basically the laziest fuck in our entire living situation. I was undecided like most freshman, but with so many girls already preparing for their futures constantly swirling around me, I looked scatterbrained and unawares when it came to what I wanted to do with my life. That was made worse as of recently, the paranoia and not wanting to leave my room. Like Hales said, I basically hadn't gone to classes all week.

Smiling at me, she bounced in with her little blond ponytail, dyed unlike mine. She kept asking about my stylist, but my pale colored locks just kind of came out that way, too lazy to do anything else. She hugged me. "Well, good. And my God, have you been secretive lately. Really, *what* happened with Bryce?"

Had she paid attention to anything but her books she might know Bryce Coventry, the guy I left that night at the club was dead. I knew *the college knew* because it was all over the Internet the next day. *"Troubled Coventry heir kills himself. Are the burdens of college stress too much?"*

They were for me, the fact I was in my bedroom and not on the way to my psych class apparent. I had that one first thing this morning.

I touched Hales's hand. "Didn't work out. Don't think I'll be dating for a while."

"Ah, shame." She pouted, putting her chin on my shoulder. "I really thought you'd get that one. He was pretty much sex on legs."

I *knew* sex on legs. I knew dark brown eyes so captivating they were almost pretty. But there was nothing "pretty" about Knight Reed. Knight Reed was a bully. Knight Reed was a tool, and he also had a complete God complex. How else did he think pushing me around and telling me what I could or could not talk about that night would come across? He was also a snob and a half with his ritzy parties and the only reason I *hadn't* said anything about that night was the same reason I was in here. He might be out there, watching me. After all, he had my phone number.

"Remember to be a good little dove."

Those words haunted me, the text message gone but their meaning still lingering in my racing heart. He'd threatened me. Basically told me to shut up and keep my head down. I'd been doing that all week, and it would no doubt ultimately be the reason I squandered away the free tuition both Mom and Ben were getting me. They'd pulled a lot of strings to let me go to this expensive school and, in Mom's case, even taken a crappy job. She was a janitor when she was way more quali-fied with her office work background. She could be working as an administrative assistant somewhere and only came here because Ben, her new husband, had gotten a job here as campus police. Even his work hadn't been able to cover my schooling, so Mom too made the sacrifice to work here, for me.

Yeah, you gotta get your ass up today.

Deciding on that, I squeezed Hales's arm, assuring her once again everything was fine and I actually was going to class today. This of course sent her through the roof, so driven like our other roommates. None of them really wanted to see me get behind, and we had gotten rather close despite being placed to live with each other. Living in the dorms at all instead of with Ben and Mom in town was another reason I was getting my shit together and going to class. I managed to get the grades enough for a partial housing stipend, but they were still filling in the gaps. I was definitely taking advantage of the situation and most assuredly letting Knight Reed win. I could go to class. Him and all his threats wouldn't scare me.

After showering, I put on a pair of shortalls and a tank, that top and shorts from the other night long buried in the trash the night I got home. My roommates actually ended up fishing them out of it, telling me they were designer, and I'd lost my mind. I let them have them because I just wanted to get rid of them in the end.

I settled for my comfort to casual clothing and tennis shoes, grabbing my bag before sprinting across the street toward campus. The buildings were all close enough that cutting through the quad got you to most classes and the rest, the transit authority. The buses ran every ten minutes in the rural Midwestern town, even more here on campus. I'd lived a lot of places over the years with my mom before she married Ben, seen a lot of things, and nothing was as nice and easy as being in a small town. The only thing that came close to Pembroke U had been when we lived in Maywood Heights, about a two hour or so drive from here. That was probably how Knight Reed and his lot ended up here, a Richie Rich school for the Richie Rich snobs.

I made it to my psych class with moments to spare, the class size about two hundred or so in the wide auditorium. Immediately, I scaled the stairs toward my normal seat in the back, and so goal-oriented, I literally made it up to the top level before I saw him.

"Remember to be a good little dove."

Those words froze me stiff, those brown-black eyes staring back at me from the top row of class. Knight had his arm draped lazily over one of the stadium seats, a black boot up on the chair in front. He literally look like a god on a throne, the rest of his freshman minions rustling around and trying to find a seat in front of him. I mean, this wasn't a freshman class, but it was a 110 elective and the basic level.

His arm dropped as I stared, and making eye contact with me, he jerked just two fingers to come his way. Plenty of seats around, I definitely had more options, but something told me if I took one, he might chase me, but not just that. Him chasing me meant he'd have to get up to do that, and something *really told me* that inconvenience might be a mistake.

Swallowing, I took quick steps but left a seat or two between us. This of course didn't matter. He eased that big body up, and once he did, he hugged that massive frame of his right up against me.

I wiggled in my seat, a harsh heat perspiring sweat down my spine and jerking my belly. Especially when Knight settled his arm across the back of *my chair* and pushed his fingers under the strap of one of my bibs. He tugged at it. "Could you dress more like a little kid?"

Definitely not needing his fashion advice, I worked my shoulder to remove his fingers. I lifted my back off my chair. "Are you even in this class?"

"No."

"Then why are you here?" I faced him, those pretty eyes with a hint of mischief boring into mine.

His hand folding over my shoulder, he brought me closer, tugging at my tank this time. "I would have assumed that was obvious." His finger played at the top of my joint, almost touching my bra strap when he reached in. "Checking on my little dove."

Like fuck he was. My hands sweaty on my bag, I reached inside, taking out my laptop to ready myself for class. Professor Hershel had already made his way in, getting ready at the podium, and I turned on my MacBook. "Do I even want to know how you know my class schedule?"

"Probably not." He played at my joint again, and when he leaned over, the heat of his lips ghosted over my top and bibs.

I sucked in a breath. "What are you doing?"

"Smelling you."

"Why?"

A shrug and he pulled back, his smile coy. "Anyone ever tell you, you smell like candy?"

"Not lately, no." I worked my shoulder away again, trying not to reveal how much I burned by what he said, did. My hands curled on my keys. "Why are you in here?"

"Like I said, checking on you. Making sure you're okay and holding up your end of the deal."

I fought myself from smirking at what deal. He told me something and I had no option but to abide by it. "You're horrible at deals, you know? Usually deals require you to have options."

"Oh, you always have options, Greer." Pulling back, his wide chest stretched beneath his T-shirt. He dashed up his eyebrows. "It's just up to you whether you want to do something stupid with them."

"Are you threatening me?"

"I don't threaten." He honed in. "But I do always get what I want."

"That sounds like a threat to me."

"Call it what you want, but that's how it is. I don't know if anyone told you, but you're in my school. You're on *my* campus, so as far as this school is concerned, that makes me your king." He paused just to flick up my chin. "Which means you, my subject, are whatever I want you to be on any given day."

A heat pooled as his fingers danced under my chin, just as much fire in his eyes as between my legs. Again, this confused me, his intimidation making me shake as much as something else. I dampened my lips. "What if I don't want to be whatever you want on any given day?"

He smiled as he pulled my lips apart, but then, it faded as he gripped my jaw, something he more than liked to do.

"Always that *mouth*," he growled, his thumb reaching and tugging my bottom lip down. "Let's hope it doesn't get you in trouble."

Trouble was nothing but him, and trouble seemed to follow me all through the rest of class and to lunch. Knight escorted me to the cafeteria in the quad, and though he opened doors and bought me food, he was nothing like a chivalrous knight. He was a demon king in his designer jeans that made his butt look like a muscular ass reel from Porn-Hub. I ate my lunch with nibbled bites while he hovered his presence over me.

"So where you been?" he asked me, *not* eating anything at all. He seemed to get more pleasure watching me, his fingers laced across the table. "For the past ten years, I mean."

Try everywhere? Grumbling, I faced anything but him. "Let's not do this."

"Do what?"

"Do *this*?" I passed a hand between us. "You sitting here making conversation with me like you care."

"I do care."

"Do you?"

He frowned. "I don't ask if I don't care."

Rolling my eyes, I stared away. "We've been all over. Moved back to the state when my stepdad got a job on campus. He and my mom both work here."

"Therefore, you go here." He leaned back. "You're lucky, you know. This is a hard school to get in to."

"Well, I got decent grades." I swung my gaze over. "What's your excuse?"

The wrong thing to say, heated eyes as he got up and came to my side of the table. He draped an arm on my other side, hugging me between him and the booth. His eyes flicked right. "Grab one of those fries."

"Why?"

He started to grab me, but then I took one. He backed off then, seeing he got what he wanted, his smile content. "Touch it to your lips. Taste it, but don't eat it."

Gazing around, I felt nothing but humiliation regardless that no one was actually looking over here. Breathing, I ran the fry across my lips.

"Slower."

"Seriously?"

His eyes heated again. "Slower."

I did, warm salt over my lips before opening my mouth.

"Only a taste."

Doing that too my tongue poked out, touching along the tip of the fry. After I was done, he grabbed my hand. "Now feed it to me."

"No."

"*Feed it*," he gritted, his fingers digging into my hand. "To me."

I scanned his eyes, completely serious as he waited. He let go, and I had about two seconds to make a decision. I could tell him to fuck off, fuck everything, and go to the police like I should have days ago. To tell them about *him*, about what he was doing to me with his sick manipulation. My stepdad was a cop for frick's sake. I should have told him.

So much warning was in Knight's eyes as he stared at me, a dare as he watched me weigh my options. This was definitely a power play here, a choice he was technically letting me make.

"…you always have options, Greer… It's just up to you whether you want to do something stupid with them."

I fed him the fry, quickly but that wasn't where this stopped. His hand grabbed mine again, and so quick, I couldn't let go in time before he pulled my finger into his mouth.

He sucked, a grin and a pop as he pulled my digit out, then chewed the food I gave him. After, he took a napkin, rubbing his mouth, and my brain radiated, my insides twisted and chest fucking heaving. I couldn't breathe.

Especially when he kissed me.

He pulled my head forward, a small kiss to my brow before standing up. He ran a thumb across my bottom lip. "Good little dove."

Good little dove… What the fuck?

And I'd played right into it, had the nerve to burn and feel his lips on my brow after he walked away. He passed my roommates on the way out, and how did I know? Because they squealed as they made their way over to me.

"My God, was that Knight Reed?" Sophie asked, her lunch tray in hand. She and the others got Chick-fil-A and immediately crowded around me. "I heard there's like a building named after him."

"After his family." Keisha squealed, pumping her little fists before facing me. "But still! Ah! Why was he here? And did we just see him kiss you? Are you dating? What the fuck?"

"We're not dating," I quickly cut, Knight at the entry doors and pounding a couple other guys' fists. They all had a silver ring on like him, but before he left, he threw an arm around a girl. He got another on his other side, and *that's* when he left, the whole party leaving the cafeteria. I frowned. "We just know each other from a long time ago."

"Um, need to know! Oh my God." Haley basically melted in her chair, another squeal before facing me. "He's so loaded. So… *hot*. My God, how could you not tell us you know him?"

No, *that man* thought he was a god, and what did that say about me? I'd let him suck my finger in front of the whole cafeteria…

Then had the nerve to get turned on by it.

CHAPTER
SIX

Knight

I grunted, spilling between Melrose's perfectly plumped lips. I fought a good dick sucking for a couple of days, but in the end, texted her.

I kept thinking about that *mouth*.

Greer had stood up to me the other day, something I wasn't particularly used to and hadn't enjoyed. Shoving my dick inside Melrose now seemed to be the only way to relieve a raging hard on that'd been recurring lately, no matter how many times I rubbed one off, the very thought of Greer and her attitude giving me a semi. A good cock suck would keep the thing at bay for a little while, better than my own hand.

At least that was what I hoped.

My eyes rolled back as Melrose finished the job, taking all my cum and running her tongue along the shaft after she was done. I fell out of her mouth with a pop, and when she lay on my bare chest, she folded her fingers. "Good?"

She didn't know how good, my hand falling to her back. I hadn't fucked her, didn't have the stamina. The moment I'd gotten her into my room, I'd forced her to her knees, modeling not the only thing this girl was good at. The girl was grade-A at giving head, something she not only loved to do but came ready whenever I texted. All girls pretty much did, but no girl gave deep throat like her. She moved off my chest to kiss me, but I pulled her back by her hair.

"Homework," I lied, easing myself up. I found my jeans and shoved them on. "Maybe next time?"

Probably not as I couldn't get Greer out of my head. I honestly didn't even know if I could get hard if I called another girl over, but the visions of Greer and those fuckable lips of hers had proved not only to get the job done but bust a nut into Melrose's mouth as easily as when I was a teenager. I had a feeling I was just biding my time. The more times I did it with Melrose, the less and less simple visions of Greer would suffice. The girl was obviously in my head, and I didn't have time for it, all this with her ridiculous. I'd checked up on her the other day mostly to keep her mouth shut, but then she'd teased me with that little mouth and the little devil in my cock got excited. He wanted to play the game, play with her.

Christ, would this girl get off my bed?

Urging Melrose, I pushed her away to shrug my shirt on. She came with me, kissing my back, but after I told her I had homework to do again, she finally got up, giving me her little pouty lips and telling me how cute I was that I was being all responsible and shit. *That alone* had me kicking her out of my fucking house. I wasn't cute, but whatever she wanted to fucking say. I let her see her way out, and after, I did grab some of my school stuff and head downstairs. I guessed Greer's comment got to me a little bit about being a dumbass, and I could technically afford to put in a little more effort when it came to school. In high school, I'd been awesome at the tech stuff, but as a business major, I didn't use any of that stuff so much now.

"You cocksuckers better not have drank all my juice," I chided, seeing some of my frat brothers on the couch. They were playing video games with a couple of girls on their laps, and I tossed my bag on a section of the couch. "Make room."

They did, groaning as they put my bag in my seat. I'd do work on the couch, but decided to take my juice in the kitchen. No one had gratefully touched it, good on them as they'd live another day.

I stamped a glass on the counter before filling it with OJ, as one of the younger brothers came into the kitchen. He was a new guy, not so much in our circle like those of us from back home, but he was cool, loyal. He had a bag of groceries with him, and when he slid a fresh bottle of OJ across the kitchen island at me, he got even more cool points. I pounded his fist. "Thanks."

"No problem. I was out so whatever."

I polished off the one, then replaced its space in the fridge with the new one, closing the door. I started to leave the kitchen before Chad got my attention again.

"I saw that girl you were talking to the other night," he said, putting his own things away in the fridge now. "That one you and Bryce were both talking to with Melrose?"

Freezing, I shifted. "Yeah? Where did you see her?"

Seeing Greer wasn't a big deal. I mean, she did go school here so whatever. Chad balled up the grocery bag, taking a beer out the fridge before closing it with his boot.

"Just saw her," he said, cracking it open on the counter. "Thought it was weird because of where she was going into. She cool? She wouldn't be trying to run her mouth about anything that went on here the other night, right?"

Not unless she was stupid. Now I was really curious about where he said she was going. "Where was she going?"

"Campus police," he said, his brew doing him right when he breathed out a refreshed sigh. He pointed a finger. "The one on the east side of campus. But it was probably nothing. She wouldn't be that stupid."

He pounded my fist again, leaving the room. I snagged my car keys off the counter, then headed out the back door. Homework could wait.

My attention was obviously needed elsewhere.

Greer

I dangled my legs from Ben's desk, dunking a dumpling into some soy sauce. I accidentally kicked a set of files, and Mom nudged me to get off my stepdad's desk before he got back.

"Honey bug, you are *not* paying attention lately," she said, eating out of her own carton of sweet and sour pork. She and I had picked up dinner for Ben tonight, something we used to do every week until more recent events.

Knowing that was all me, I frowned. "Sorry. Accident."

Her brow lifted behind her carton before Ben came over in his cop uniform, a few cans of assorted soda beverages in his arms. I see he'd raided the precinct's vending machines tonight. He grinned, putting out his display for us. "I got Sprite, Coke, and something that isn't name brand. I think it's basically Mountain Dew?"

Pointing to that, I took it but didn't open it, tapping my finger against the can while Mom chose the can of Sprite. Ben opened it for her before pecking her and sitting back down behind his desk, the two of them absolutely adorable. I'd admit I had been weird at first when my mom told me she wanted to start dating again, and when she had, it'd been really fucking weird. She went through a few losers before this guy came around, Ben actually pretty cool.

Especially for a cop.

He took really good care of us, care of my mom, and

lounging back, he tossed an arm behind Mom's folding chair. He jerked a chin at me. "Something wrong with the dumplings?"

I frowned. "No, why?"

I followed their gazes to the dumpling that currently dripped soy sauce on the campus precinct's floor and cursed, falling to the floor with some paper towels. The curse got me a chide from my mom, who was well aware I'd been swearing since middle school. Hell, she'd been doing it with me until Ben came along. He came from old family values, i.e., a stick in the mud, but he was sweet, kind despite his need for nightly family dinners when I'd been in school and a curfew that saw me home by nine o'clock every night even when I'd been a senior. I shook my head. "Sorry."

"No big." Ben headed to the floor with me, getting some Kleenex from his desk. Between the two of us, we got it up, and using some of Mom's hand sanitizer, we got the stickiness away too. Ben balled everything both he and I had up before trashing it and returning to his chair. He grinned again. "So you gonna let your mom and I in on why you're so out of it?"

"Out of it?"

Mom tapped me with her sneaker, in her own uniform with the Pembroke University's insignia on her polo. She'd just come off a shift before picking me up so we could get dinner for Ben during his evening shift. "Yeah, or why you've been missing family dinners?"

I hadn't gone to one since this whole thing with Knight. I shrugged. "Nothing. Just busy with school."

"Hardly." She frowned. "Until recently, your Instagram account has been nothing but you partying."

I frowned now. "You've been stalking me?"

"Actually, Greer, I believe it's called parenting?" Ben raised a chopstick, waggling his brown eyebrows at his joke before feeding my mom some kung pao chicken. The two may be adorable, but really disgusting sometimes. I mean, it was my mom... He turned my way. "Everything, okay? You really do seem different."

"Yeah, baby." She folded her hand over my knee. "Maybe it's *too much* partying? If it's a problem, we can move you back home next semester. That's okay, you know?"

God, no. Between the two of them, they might actually try to give me a curfew or some shit. I shook my head. "It's not a big deal. Just stressful stuff with school."

"Well, I only did some college, dear, but I think this way you're acting is weird. Even for you." She nudged me with a smile. "Tell us about it."

"There's nothing to tell." Only everything, the fact that I had a beautiful stalker the size of military vehicle threatening my life whenever he saw fit. I hadn't seen him since lunch that day, but that didn't mean I wouldn't see Knight Reed again. The campus was only so big, and he, well, was fucking large. I poked at my food. "Actually, there is something."

"Yes." Excitement dancing in my mom's eyes, she scooted closer, Ben too with interest and I rolled my eyes.

"Remember Knight Reed?" I asked, being passive about it. I dunked another dumpling before popping it into my mouth. "That boy from Maywood Heights?"

"I do." She frowned and when Ben looked at her, she shrugged. "He's a boy who lived at one of the houses I used to clean. Greer and I lived at his grandfather's estate for a while. I was one of their live-in housekeepers."

"Ah..." Ben lifted his head before his eyes flashed. "His grandpa isn't Gerald Reed, is he?"

My chest tightened at the thought he knew anything about the Reeds. "Yeah, why?"

Ben lounged back, his fingers threading across his chest. "Well, we have him to thank for our spanking new uniforms. Gear?" He flashed his utility belt, and I supposed his uniform did appear new. Honestly, I wouldn't even know the difference since I didn't really pay that much attention. Ben smiled. "I heard his grandson goes to Pembroke. Do you two know each other closely?"

"No, why would you ask that?" I said this too fast, enough for them to both notice when they narrowed their eyes. I pushed around my hair. "I mean, not particularly. I ran into him."

"Did you? How is he?" Mom asked, and though I maybe had ill will toward Knight and his grandpa for firing her and making us homeless all those years ago, my mom wasn't nearly as petty. She'd moved on, and when the whole thing went down, I hadn't recalled her really being mad at all. If anything, she'd just been more sad. "Greer?"

I jumped. "Yeah?"

She smiled. "What did he have to say? How is he now? He used to be such the little adult back then, Ben. Seriously, I'd never seen a child direct a house just like his grandpa. He liked things a certain way, a terribly bossy little thing."

More like entitled as fuck. Dampening my lips, I said nothing. "Sorry, and it's nothing. I just ran into him."

"Are you sure—"

"I said it's nothing." And really, this whole thing was fucking stupid, coming here to eat with them. For all I knew, he was still watching me. I gathered my things, tossing my trash before reaching over and hugging Ben. "Thanks for the food."

It'd been on his tab, always, and after he returned the hug, I reached and kissed my mom, doing the same with a hug.

She rubbed my back. "Okay. You got homework or something? It's not that late."

Yeah, that. I nodded. "And sorry. I'll try to do the dinner thing more."

They both smiled at me, but mine couldn't really be full. Knight Reed was in my freaking head, and the way Ben talked about him and his rich grandpa, you'd think he was one of the Reeds' biggest fans. Maybe he was, blinded just like Haley, Keisha, and Sophie had been. Even my mom held no ill will toward the Reeds, myself the minority.

Mom offered to drive me back to my dorm, but since the transit authority ran every ten minutes and I had a pass, I just hopped on, holding the bar on the short trip home. Getting off at my stop, I just wanted a shower and found my room-mates belly down with their textbooks on the floor. I'd missed our nightly study session tonight due to family dinner.

"Hey," I said, passing quickly through the room. I didn't really want to talk to anyone, just wanted to shower, and was in and out of the room before they'd barely been able to say hi. Sophie called down the hall for me, and as I opened the door, she said his name.

"Knight's waiting for you in your room," she said, but it was too late.

My hand had already been on the knob, steps made to go inside, and I couldn't even stop my momentum if I tried. I was jerked inside my bedroom by a hand that encased my entire wrist, and once pulled in, the door was slammed behind me.

I was forced up against it, a knee between my legs and warm breath breezed against my ear. Knight Reed smelled like heaven laced with something hellish, the devil in designer threads staring back at me.

"Big mistake, little dove," he said, dragging his nose along the shell of my ear. He put hands on either side of my head. "Going to the cops?"

CHAPTER
SEVEN

Greer

My heart beat like a jackrabbit, Knight's lips brushing my earlobe. "Stop."

"Or what?" he breathed, a smile in his voice. "You'll tell on me? Go back to the campus police?"

"I didn't tell—"

His hand slammed the door, and I jumped, quivering between his arms. What the hell was he doing?

He curled a finger against my throat. "I own the campus, baby. Fuck, own the *real* police."

"I didn't…" Braving up, I stood tall. My jaw tightened. "I didn't say anything to them, asshole."

His chuckle dry, he angled a look away, a fake out before his hand folded around my throat. He squeezed ever so slightly, making it so hard to breath.

"You're strangling me." More so panic than his actual hand, more so fear than anything else and the madness in his eyes I'd seen too many times before. This guy was seriously crazy, *mental*, and here I was stuck in a room with him. I reached back for the door, trying to turn the knob, and his hand found mine.

He pulled it away, my lips trembling.

"I'll scream."

"And I dare you." His lips came closer, his knee raising and pressing against the heat between my legs. I gasped, and his smile widened, his fingers tipping down my chin. "This turning you on, dove?" he asked me, hovering his nose over my cheek. "Turning you on like it is me."

He pressed his big body against me for emphasis, his cock rock hard against my tummy, and my belly jumped. He was hard for me, *steel* and getting off on this.

My eyes watered. "You're sick."

"Am I?" His knee pulsed my mound again, his thumb tapping my throat. Reaching, he grabbed hold of my thigh and curled it around his hip, his knee rubbing friction against my pussy lips. "So what does that make you since you're riding *my damn* knee?"

I wasn't. At least, I *thought* I wasn't. I honestly didn't have too much experience with this, a man making me do this. His knee between my legs did feel good, though, hence more of that confusion in my head. Hell, we were both messed up. Completely—fucked.

I gripped his arms, pulling. "Let go of me."

"Not until you tell me why you decided to do something stupid. I told you to keep your mouth shut about the other night."

The fact that he did know about my visit to see my stepdad told me he had been watching me. He had been stalking me or at least had someone tailing me. I swallowed. "I didn't. My stepdad Ben is campus police. I told you he and my mom work here on campus."

"Not helping your case, Greer." His hand replaced his knee, and before I knew it, he was gripping my pussy.

I called out, my mound rubbing his hand. I couldn't stop it. It felt good…

And damn did he know it.

He grinned at me, his tongue wetting his lips as his hand went from a grip to a pinch. He pinched my lips with three digits, his handsome smirk one of the devil.

"I like you like this," he said, his voice husky and aroused. "Submitting to me. Knowing your place." He honed in, his mouth covering my ear. "Just wait until I have my dick in you."

"Dream on." I said the words, but they proved to be just as rough and aroused as his own. I loved his hands on me, loved how hard and rough they were. They matched who he was to the nines.

Fuck, I really am fucked up.

I closed my eyes as he pinched my earlobe between his teeth, tugging just once. "So how much does dear old stepdad know? I told you. I own them all."

The Reeds sure did, and tonight had proved that when I'd gone over there. I'd barely mentioned Knight and his grandpa and *my* stepdad was telling me about them. I gripped his wrist, hand still around my throat. "He doesn't know anything."

"Don't lie to me, Greer."

"I'm not. I swear. My mom and I just took him dinner tonight. We usually do it every week."

"And what does she know?" His gaze panned and found me. Using my neck, he forced my head back to touch the door. "What have you told her?"

"Nothing." True fear this time, yes, at threatening Ben but even more at my mom. She wasn't a part of this, neither of them having anything to do with this. I shook my head. "She doesn't know anything. I swear."

"Swear to who, Greer?" he asked, his hand reaching up and unhooking one of my bib straps. I didn't wear shortalls today, but a romper. The strap falling before he went to the other. "Swear to me."

He unfastened that one too, a tug and the material fell down to my ankles. His hand reached between my legs again. Pinching me hard through my underwear.

"Knight, stop." But I didn't want him to stop, my arms hooking around and bracing his big back. I rode his hand and wasn't even reluctant about it. I wanted his touch, to feel him pulsating inside me.

His nose ran down my neck as he did, and letting go of my throat, he braced my hip. "Want me to make you come, Greer?" he asked me, his voice velvet and gravelly. "Want me to show this pussy who's in charge?"

So dirty, but the threat made me grip him harder. He picked me up, tugging my romper right off my legs and leaving my shoes on. That quick he was trying to get this done, tossing me on the bed before working his shirt off.

He was chiseled marble, perfect in all the right sections. His abs actually looked like a fucking chocolate bar, each section a clean line. I wanted to touch him, but he wouldn't let me, grappling my hands with one fist before using the other to tear my panties clean off my body.

He balled them up, giving them a lick before stuffing them in his pocket. His eyes were completely wild, and using my own hand, he stuck them between my legs.

"Knight…" I didn't have time to tell him I'd never done this before. Well, at least with a guy around. Whenever I pleasured myself, I'd very much been alone, but he didn't wait around for explanation. He merely entered me with my own fingers, using his own digits to strum me, and I started to scream so loud he had to cover my mouth.

"Quiet, Dove," he said, his tongue lapping at my lips but he didn't kiss me. He just teased me, the one completely in control here, and he wanted me to know. He didn't kiss me unless he wanted to, made me come because that's what *he* wanted to do. I had no control here at all, my sex bucking wildly against our hands.

"So hot," he said, and with his tongue he wet a circle over my tank top, my nipple diamond hard even through my bra. He tugged it with his teeth, actually groaning, and I scratched his back. He chuckled. "God, you're a freak like me."

I hadn't thought I was before this, but here I was, fucking myself and letting him do it. My eyes rolled back, Knight taking me to the brink, and that's when he kissed me, full on with his tongue inside my mouth. He tasted like heaven, sweet with that rough edge. He tasted like power, and I breathed in his life force, his hand pulling mine out to replace with his own.

He fucked me wildly after that, stroking in and out while his thumb flicked my clit. They matched the strokes of his tongue tasting mine, and before I knew it, I was pooling wildly around his digits.

He had me come so hard down from the high, my lips between his teeth and after he found my eyes, stared right in them.

I think for the first time.

His hand left me after that, quick before reaching over and tugging his shirt on.

I sat up, completely confused. I was naked from the waist down, lying by myself with arousal between my legs. My fingers were sticky, my own cum, and Knight barely looked at me before getting up and heading toward the door.

"Knight…" I had no idea why I'd said his name, but it'd been enough to make him stop.

He turned, his dark eyes like something from behind hell's gates. "Clean yourself up, Greer," he said, picking up a towel off the top of my laundry pile. He tossed it at me. "Your whore is showing a little."

Completely frozen, I watched as he slammed the door, making me jump once again. Tears in my eyes, I did clean myself, trying not to cry as I put my clothes back on. He'd called me a whore.

And basically tried to make me look like one.

CHAPTER
EIGHT

Knight

The dumbbells clanked to the floor when I dropped them, Royal's eyes twitching wide at me mid-curl. He smirked. "My gym piss you off or something?"

We always used his since he had his own personal one at his high rise apartment. He didn't live on campus or the frat, preferring the city. The frat had a nice gym too, but the privacy of Royal's was better. No need to have to elbow a motherfucker for some weights.

"Shut the fuck up." My ass was in a mood today, clearly. Hence, why I was at the gym and not actually hitting a dude. An even worse scenario would be me anywhere in the vicinity of Greer, someone who'd given me the ultimate head fuck. I'd kissed her. Hell, but worse. I'd fucking liked it to the point where I hadn't wanted to stop, and that drove me crazy. I'd wanted to teach her a lesson about talking back.

Not feel something for her.

Well, I think I proved to correct all that, calling her a whore and shit. She obviously wasn't one. Fuck, the way I'd touched her it'd been like she *hadn't* been touched, but I'd be hard-pressed to believe that. She may dress in her little kid overalls, but kitten was all fire cat. She knew how to use what she had to drive a guy crazy, and I couldn't possibly be the first.

Throwing the dumbbell this time, I got more than a look from Royal, but he did spot me when I asked him to come over. He eased up on the weight on each side, and I gave him a look that told him I'd kick his ass if he didn't stop playing around.

Chuckling, he added more weight, getting behind the bench when I lay down. He helped me with the bar, but then I didn't need him, his hand under while I lifted and lowered it.

"So what kind of flowers do you like?" he asked, asking me fucking questions when I had the weight of like three dudes hovering over me. He smirked, helping me put the weight back on the bar. "I just want to know what to have at your funeral since you're clearly trying to kill yourself today."

Flipping him off, I sat up, finally fucking winded. It took that and twice my regular workout today to do it, but I'd accomplished it. Royal went over to the gym's cooler, tossing me a water and towel before getting the same for himself. I downed half. "Just need to tire myself out."

"Clearly." He sat across from me on another weight bench. "Wanna let me in on what's going on?"

Try hell fucking no. I guzzled the rest of the bottle before he rolled his eyes.

He snapped the towel at my knee. "Are were really going to do this toxic masculinity shit right now? It's really okay for two dudes to talk about serious shit, you know? Not really a thing?"

I sneered at words clearly from his girl coming out of his mouth. I smirked. "You can tell December she can rest easy now knowing that she's gotten you in touch your feelings."

The fucker kicked at my kneecap, and I nearly fell off the weight bench, bent over in pain. His eyebrows dancing in response, Royal took a drink of water. If he wanted to prove something, he did there. He put out a finger. "Whatever. Just trying to help."

"Well, don't." I stood, throwing my fists at a punching bag, and once again, he spotted me, going behind and hugging it. I got a few jabs before I took in a breath and looked at him. "Remember that girl the other night?"

"What girl?"

I gave him a look like it was obvious. "The one you brought December's clothes for."

"Yeah?" My punch sending him back a bit, he hugged the bag again. "What about her? She running her mouth?"

Just like me, that need to maintain the status quo serious amongst the brothers. Royal no longer wore his Court ring, the thing around his girl's neck now, but Court blood ran hard through him. It was something that probably wouldn't ever leave, and the only reason December had the ring was because of a statement he was making to everyone. He shared that part of himself with someone else, the two of them bonded.

My own ring in my pocket, I jabbed once, then twice. "She's not. Not that I know of anyway."

"Then what's the issue?"

Nothing but the sounds of my fists hitting the bag, as hard as I could, until I tired myself out again. "She's the same girl from when we were kids, you know?" I stated, then stood. "The one who used to live at my house?"

"Wait. The one you killed that dog over?"

I froze, a history I'd never actually dissected with him, but clearly, he knew why I'd asked him to help me take down Old Man Peabody's dog that day. The thing had been chasing Royal and me, as well as other kids in the neighborhood for years. Almost got us a few times too…

But it hadn't been until Greer moved into my house that I actually chose to do something about it. It had gotten her that day, a bite right at her ankle, and I'd snapped. Royal and I had just happened to be out playing in the woods, heard her screams.

I hadn't told Royal back then why we should take out the dog, but I guess I hadn't needed to. My friend, too fucking observant.

"Sure," I could only say now, not letting that girl have any more power over me than she already did. "I've been keeping an eye on her to make sure she doesn't talk. I guess it's just been getting annoying."

The understatement of the year how much she truly got under my skin. Some days, I just wanted to choke the shit out of her, others stick my cock inside her *while* I choked the shit out of her. It was some kind of evil and kind of did scare me a little. Royal and I came from some mad bullshit where he and I grew up, and I didn't want to necessarily be like all the evil that came out of Maywood Heights. There were things a guy had to do sometimes to keep order, yes. But there were other times things could definitely go too far, something Royal himself could say.

After all, his father was in prison.

He let me continue to exhaust myself, saying nothing for a while before asking to switch off. I did, spotting him.

He punched. "So what are you going to do about her?" he asked. "You going to do something?"

"I don't know."

He smiled. "You wanna do something?"

Again, I didn't know. More punches, and after, he stood tall. He touched a fist to the bag. "You know you don't have to be so fucking rigid. If you wanna talk to a girl, you should just fucking talk to her."

Wait. How did this go from me needing to control Greer to

needing to talk to her? I shook my head. "That's not what I said."

"No." He picked up his towel, wiping his face before tugging it over his shoulders. "But that's what you meant, right?"

He thought he was so fucking smart, didn't he? I scrubbed through sweaty hair. "Fuck, no. She just has a mouth on her, and I need to know what to do about it."

"How about you just handle it? Like you did with that dog?" He nudged me. "You seemed to know what to do then."

I swore to God I couldn't talk to this guy. I rolled my eyes. "Sorry I even mentioned it."

He cut me off when I started to walk away. "I'm just saying when it comes to girls, sometimes there's shit there that you just don't see. They make things complicated. Make you want things you don't understand."

I frowned. "That's not what's happening here."

"Whether it is or not, you don't have to push away every woman that comes walking around you." He frowned suddenly, his expression sad. "I mean, when was the last time you saw your mom? Visited her?"

We *definitely* weren't talking about that, my mom, and he was totally out of line here. My eyebrows narrowed. "You're reaching."

"Am I?" He pulled the towel off his neck. "Or are you lying? Lying to yourself?"

I wasn't lying to anyone, and the only thing that needed to happen between Greer and me was *me* showing her, her proper place. I hadn't taught her enough of a lesson the other night, and not only was I going to correct that issue, there'd be no mistake where we stood. She was nothing but pussy, nothing but *mouth*, and I'd make her see that, done with the mindfuck.

It was time to turn the tides.

CHAPTER
NINE

Greer

I was falling asleep in class. Hell, I fell asleep in all my classes lately.

Psych 110 no exception, I curled up in the stadium seat, Professor Hershel lecturing across the front stage. These days getting any kind of sleep only happened in my classes anyway, the result of constant paranoia and stress when it came to Knight. I figured if class already started, the door closed and all focus in the room on my professor, he wouldn't dare come in.

At least that had been my theory.

It'd been working so far so I took advantage of the time, fifty some odd minutes of sleep better than nothing at all. I obviously couldn't sleep at the dorm, not with what happened in my own bedroom and mere steps away from my roommates. They hadn't heard anything at all that'd been going on in my bedroom. Not that it sounded like I was at all in trouble in the end anyway. I completely gave my body over to Knight—willingly.

That was what scared me the most.

I would have done more had he taken it there, more because I wanted to. He left me humiliated in the end, damaged beyond repair, and I hated him. Hated him so much more than before this whole thing started. He was just as crazy as he had been when we were kids, just as hurtful. I needed to stay away from him, my sole focus, and privacy these days was nothing but a silent killer. Having people around and not being in the open was better for me. At least if he found me in my classes, he wouldn't have an opportunity to take advantage.

I wouldn't do anything fucking stupid either.

I jumped as Professor Hershel dismissed class, everyone gathering up their things. I got mine too, heading down the auditorium stairs and across the room. I passed the professor's podium along the way, and he stopped me, waving me over.

After studying something on his podium, he looked up at me, frowning. "Greer Michaelson, right?"

"Yes, Professor," I stated, slowing my strides and wondering what this was about. He'd never acknowledged me before, this class way too big. His teaching assistants usually only talked to us individually on recitation days.

The professor tucked his stuff in his bag. "I know we don't take participation into account when it comes to grades for this class, but if I catch you sleeping again, I might have to. It's wasting your time and mine."

Completely caught, my heart raced. I adjusted my bag. "I'm sorry, sir. I just haven't been getting enough sleep lately."

"I'm sure you and half your classmates. This is college." Closing his messenger bag's flap, he slid it over his shoulder. "What I say stands. Don't let it happen again; otherwise, your grade will be affected."

Knowing he was serious, I nodded, heading out the room

with the rest of my classmates. Completely humiliated again, I covered my face, so over this whole thing.

He's affecting me, and he's not even here.

I was blowing myself up now, my hopes for an education. Even though I was undecided, I'd eventually know what I wanted to do with my life and couldn't afford to take this class over. I might have to pay out of pocket for that, and both Ben *and* Mom would have my ass. They'd worked so hard for me to go to school here.

Feeling terrible, I headed across campus to get some lunch and frankly, reevaluate my life at this point. My phone buzzed, and my stomach tossed for only a few seconds before seeing it was my roommates, a group text, and thank God nothing from Knight Reed.

Sophie: You guys want to meet for pizza for lunch?

Keisha: Sweet! Green Street sound, okay? They got the best pizza places over there.

Haley: Love it. Let's just wait until we hear from Greer. I'm close and it'll only take me a minute to get over to that area.

Same for me, and though I didn't feel like socializing, *socializing* was exactly what I needed to do. More power in numbers after all.

Me: Sounds good. The Cheezery sound okay?

It was the best place on Green Street, and since they all agreed, that's where I headed. It took me a little longer than expected to get over there, I guess dragging my feet, and by the time I actually got over to the restaurant, my friends were already in the booth. I spotted them easily upon entering.

Mostly because they weren't by themselves.

Knight had his huge ass body tucked between Sophie and Haley, his arms basically around both of them. He had his wingspan draped behind the back of the booth, so yeah, he had his arms *all* over them, and the moment he spotted me, he tipped his chin. This got the girls' attention, all of them popping up and waving at me. They looked only too giddy to have Knight Reed basically all over them, and something told me Keisha would have been a part of the sandwich too if he had another side to hug.

"Greer!"

They all said it together, but the only one truly smiling at me with mad delight was Knight himself. He was playing a new game here, easily psychological warfare, and since I was spotted by my friends, I couldn't so easily walk away.

My stomach clenched as I gripped my bag, coming over and squeezing in next to Keisha. Knight dropped his arms from around the girls after that, sitting up, and the absence definitely hadn't kept my roommates at bay. Hales and Soph hugged up on his big body like he was their life-force, grinning up at him like he was a member from a K-pop group.

"What's going on?" I asked, treading lightly here. I lay my bag on the seat of my other side, Haley leaning forward.

"Can you believe Knight was eating lunch too?" she stated, her voice way higher than it usually was. "Right over there."

She pointed to a group of guys just as big and as arrogant-looking as Knight was, talking amongst each other with their arms filled with just as many girls as Knight had when I came over. The girls swarmed these guys like locusts, but for whatever reason *this* one in particular stalked me.

"Came over to say hi," Knight said, hand tapping the table. "Recognized your friends."

This made them all giggle like four-year-olds, Haley and Sophie hugging Knight even more. In return, he dropped his arms back around them again, and I swore to God, Haley had actual drool dripping out of her mouth when his bicep merely brushed the back of her head.

"So naturally, you invited yourself to sit with us," I said, expression serious.

Knight leaned forward. "Naturally."

"We figured it'd be okay." Keisha exchanged a glance between Knight and me. "He asked if you were coming, and since you knew him, we thought…"

They figured it'd be okay. My insides were swirling so badly I wasn't sure if I could keep down anything, let alone order pizza. I started to make up some excuse, that Knight shouldn't inconvenience himself by sitting with us, but then I noticed his finger. The tip of it looped right around Haley's blond locks unbeknownst to her knowledge. He was playing with her and, in turn, playing with me.

My mouth dried. "Of course it's fine." I shifted in my seat, and only after did Knight drop his arms to his sides. He placed his hands in his lap, his muscled biceps squished between two girls a fraction of his size. His bulging arms shifted beneath his coal black T-shirt, matching his dark eyes, and I tried not to look at them as I grabbed a menu.

"Actually, already ordered for the table, Greer. On me."

Of course he had, the ass.

Knight grinned. "Meat lover's all around."

"Too bad," I said, shrugging. "I'm a vegetarian."

"Really?" Knight sat back, fingers moving to his lips. "Weird, since you were scarfing down all that chicken with your fries the other day at lunch."

My nails dug into my thigh. "Recent development."

He smirked, but did wave the waitress over. Her gaze too poured over Knight's body like she'd never seen a member of the opposite sex before, and I rolled my eyes, Knight's grin widening. "A personal pan cheese pizza please for the little dove over there with the white hair."

Freezing at the nickname he gave me, I stayed silent, shrinking in my seat after the waitress added to the order and left. Keisha touched my shoulder. "Um, *cute* nickname."

Knight shrugged. "She hates it."

"I wouldn't." Haley folded her hands and rested her chin

on them, Knight's smile light as the others *and* I gave her a look. She sat up. "What? It is cute."

Hardly, and crossing my arms, I stiffened up more. I wanted to be anywhere but here right now, but was clearly stuck for the time being. The conversation moved on when Haley started it, but before I knew it, I was being pulled right back in.

"Knight was telling us about how your mom used to work at his house," she said, bouncing her shoulders. "And, Greer, you never told us you guys *lived* together."

For all of like a minute before he'd gotten my mom fired over that dog thing, the sicko. I frowned. "Yeah, it wasn't for very long."

"How was that? I mean…" Keisha sat back. "Sounds fun."

"Never really saw Greer too much," Knight said, dashing up dark eyebrows. "She tended to keep to herself."

"More like got lost in his house," I returned, my frown deepening. "It was big enough."

Knight wet his lips before glancing at the girls. "She's right. It wasn't for very long."

"What happened?" Sophie asked, and by then, our drinks had come. She sipped her cola. Knight started to answer, but then I grabbed my drink.

"Something having to do with a *dog*, wasn't it, Knight?" I asked, his eyes smoldering. There was a definite dare in there, one I probably should heed, but with him pinned between my roommates I found myself not caring. "He likes to torture and kill them."

Silence, full on besides the outside chatter and fifties swing music from the pizzeria's jukebox. I sucked down my Coke before Keisha's elbow nudged my shoulder.

"Oh my God, nice one, Greer!" she chanted, obviously thinking I was joking. Awkwardly, she started to laugh, and the others quickly joined in, obviously wanting to believe I was joking.

Amongst the laughter, Knight swirled around his beer bottle, his eyes flicking coldly at me before taking a sip. He wiped his mouth with his finger. "Always one for jokes with that *mouth*, dove. Maybe you should do stand-up."

Maybe I should, staring him down now that I had the confidence. He couldn't do anything in this booth, intimidate me or otherwise, and though I knew I should probably tread lightly, he'd hurt me. He'd *called me a whore*, and those words radiated through my mind in a dark haze. I wanted to hurt him back, punish him, but at the moment I was gridlocked too. My roommates around, I couldn't really do anything either, so I sat there, the two of us in a stand off. Eventually, our pizzas came, a cheese personal pan sliding in front of me. Sophie eased out of the booth to go wash her hands and the others split a pizza that made my mouth water. I really did love meat lover's, but was obviously too stubborn to do anything about that now.

"Cheese not tickling your fancy, Greer?" A cool expression across the table. Knight flicked up his chin. "You're hardly touching your pizza."

"Just needs a little pepper." I reached for it, but knocked it off the table. I started to ease out of the booth to get it, but Knight stopped me, bending over his big body and getting the shaker himself.

He returned it to the table, but didn't rise all the way, fishing beneath the table for something. All too coolly, he rose with a hand full of my calf, and before I could say anything, Sophie returned.

"What did I miss?" she asked, Knight's eyes darkening as he pulled off my flip-flop beneath the table. He tossed it to the floor, staring at me and with the others devouring their pizza, they said nothing.

"Um," I started, large fingers pulsing up to the back of my knee. Knight squeezed, rubbing the pads of his thumbs over and over above my knee before his fingers pushed up and gripped my thigh. He picked up then, massaging me and before I knew it, he was setting my bare foot right on his crotch. I jumped. "Er, um…"

"You alright there, Greer?" A smirk from the son of a bitch sitting across from me, his eyes dancing with gleeful delight as he lounged back and let me feel his cock. He was rock hard through his jeans, his dark gaze simmering on his side of the table. He wet his lips. "You're looking a little bothered."

"Yeah, Greer. You okay?" Hales was staring at me, all the girls staring at me. Meanwhile, Knight was rubbing my toes against his hard on, his eyes hazing as he attempted to bring me back to a familiar place. One where he'd called me a whore and I'd not only let him get away with it, but had actually cried that night. He'd embarrassed me.

He wouldn't do it again.

A grunt when I jabbed my foot right into his balls, his eyes shrinking as he let go of my foot, and I maneuvered it back into my flip-flop. Pushing away my pizza, I grabbed my things. "I just remembered I have a lot of homework to do."

"Greer?"

I ignored Keisha and got up, leaving my pizza behind. Knight said he'd pay so I hadn't bothered leaving any cash. I left that room and table so quick and hadn't thought about the repercussions until I hit the bus stop to head back to my dorm. I got a text then, one that made my stomach absolutely sick.

Knight: I hope to God that little stunt you pulled just now was worth it. And good luck getting me out of your life now. This isn't over until I say it is.

CHAPTER
TEN

Greer

Knight proved to make good on his threat. Because not only did I find him at the dorm later that night, but he had friends with him, two huge guys about the size of himself. I caught Haley, Sophie, and even Keisha, who was hugely into taking her bedtime seriously, hanging out with them all. They all sat on or around the couch, partying away with a game system, snacks, and music blasting all around them. Knight hadn't come for me, but he basically had, his eyes glaring coolly at me as I cut across the room. I'd heard the music, the only reason I came out to see what was up.

"Hey there, dove." He once again had one of my room-mates squished into his side, Haley, with his arm stretched across the back of the couch behind her. His dark eyebrows dashed up. "Come out to join us?"

I definitely hadn't, completely disgusted, and Haley barely noticed me upon entering *or* leaving the room. She was too obsessed with Knight Reed. All of my roommates were. Belly down, Keisha and Sophie let these two gargantuan-size guys that Knight had brought show them how to play the Xbox they'd brought when my friends definitely didn't play Xbox. Like stated before, they were too serious about school.

Scoffing, I slammed the door, a sheer panic at the turn of events. Somehow things had shifted from me keeping quiet about what I saw that night at the frat to *this*, Knight Reed completely invading my life. My phone buzzed in my pocket and I reached for it.

Knight: Night one, little dove. You ready?

I threw my phone on the bed, forcing in a scream. Burrowing into my bedding, I pulled the sheets over my head.

The music only got louder.

Night one turned into every night that week, every damn night, and the more evenings Knight accrued the more people he brought, guys and girls. My dorm room was turning into the hottest spot to be at in the freshman dormitory, and I'd even caught a few of the building's resident assistants frequenting through, wanting to see what was up when they were supposed to be keeping order. The whole thing was madness, and the whole time I'd taken to nothing but barricading myself into my room. I had to. The last time I went out, I'd caught actually Haley *on* Knight's lap instead of under his arm.

He'd cradled her hip, barely looking at me when I left to go get dinner that night, but he'd definitely seen me. Nothing but a devious smirk curled his lips as he braced Haley's hip and brought her closer. He played Xbox around her, the two of them peas in a pod. I'd feigned nothing but annoyance when I snapped the door closed, but something had my heart racing and laying my head back against the door. Something had me gripping my dorm keys like a lifeline, and whatever it was, I didn't fucking like it. Knight Reed was nothing but sin, *cancer*, and fuck, did I hate him.

Fuck.

I went to bed that night like I had most nights, no sleep and nothing at all allowing me to focus. I was angry. I was frustrated, but not only could I do nothing about it, I was sure I'd get protests if I did try to do something. The other girls clearly wanted him and his friends around, so what did it matter what I wanted? I just had to hope one day Knight might get over his little obsession with me and torturing my life, move onto something else, and I thought that's what I had by that Saturday. The dorm was miraculously empty, but I definitely hadn't questioned it and decided to take full advantage of the fact when I brought my school things out and set them up in the living area. I wasn't failing all my classes yet, but was definitely on my way. I was still sleeping in most of my classes where I could get away with that, and so behind in psych it wasn't even funny. I'd actually failed the last quiz entirely.

Completely Knight Reed's fault, I grumbled over my textbook, trying to Google some of these vocabulary terms to get some clarity. If I didn't start understanding some of this shit, I couldn't use *any of this shit* for the term paper that was coming due. It was worth half my grade in combination with my final exam, so I really needed to start getting my crap together. I was finally kinda starting to get some of it when some giggling behind me caused me to stop. It drifted out of one of the girl's closed bedrooms, a deeper laugh right behind, and I closed my eyes.

A squeak of the bed, and my stomach's contents basically filled my throat, my fists curled over laptop keys. I was shaking as the door creaked open and a landmass filled Haley's door frame, Knight coming out of her room with tousled hair and his muscles stretching a T-shirt to the brink of its seams. It pulled taut over his massive chest, especially when he stretched, working his shoulders and back like he'd been laying down. He noticed me right away, of course, smirking before closing Haley's door. I didn't see her, but that must have been her inside, giggling…

Ignoring the fact that I cared something about that, I eased back behind my laptop monitor, Knight casually cutting past me. He'd taken it upon himself to make himself at home over the past few days. I mean, he'd basically solidified himself as a fifth roommate outside of paying rent. Heading over to the fridge in the kitchen across from me, he opened the door. "Working hard, Greer?"

No thanks to him. I said nothing, scrolling through my screens. Peeking above my monitor, I watched as Knight opened a carton of milk and downed the whole thing, his Adam's apple working the whole thing down, and rolling my eyes, I forced myself to concentrate on my work. There was no going to my room now that he was here. He'd might say something about that, poke at me more than he already did, and I was so damn tired of him getting the upper hand when it came to my life. In fact, it freakin' maddened me, more of his psychological warfare he was clearly playing here. He was winning this game between us, but hell if I'd ever let him know how much it was bothering me.

"Going over vocabulary terms," I said causally. I clicked around. "You know, since that's what people do in college? Go to classes and actually work?"

A chuckle as he closed the fridge. He crushed the carton with a hand, tossing it in the trash, and when he came over, I shook my head.

"Hope you'll be buying another one of those." He'd been eating us out of house and home too, like seriously a vacuum. He and his friends consumed food like locusts, but the difference between us and them was that they could afford to do shit like that. My tuition may be taken care of by Ben and Mom, but my food budget wasn't. He and his friends were bleeding us dry, and as far as I knew, my other roommates hadn't fared better on scholarships and grants themselves.

"I'm good for it." Knight hugged his heat up against my side, tilting my screen back to read it. "Psych, huh? Sounds fun."

"Don't you have stuff to do?" I pulled the screen back, another goddamn chuckle rolling its gravelly tones into my ear. I shook my head. "Other people to bother? Sounds like you and Haley were having fun."

Annoyance pricked at me when I heard an octave raise my voice, and even more when Knight's arms pulled around me. My heart leaped. "What are you doing?"

"Nothing. Just trying to hear it, your jealousy…" he said, his nose running along the shell of my ear. His biceps hugged my shoulders. "I mean, if you want me all to yourself, Greer. You just gotta ask."

"I don't want you." I simmered, my body heat rising like three hundred. More of his games, more of his evil. I pulsed. "I hate you."

"Do you?" His teeth tugged at my earlobe this time, his breath wintry and cool. He hugged my body with his big arms and hands. "Wish I actually believed that."

But I did, so much it made me blind. Made me *crazy*, and even more that no matter how much I wanted to push him away, I wanted to tug him right back to me, his heat and his draw making me just as mad as he clearly was. This was nothing but a game to him, but for whatever reason, my own heart couldn't get the reality check. I shoved at his hold, laughter in my ear when he let go of my earlobe. My jaw worked. "Get off me. I need to study."

"Sure."

"I do." I elbowed him for emphasis, and though he did back off, he smiled. My nostrils flared. "I'm on the cusp of failing half my classes thanks to you and your nightly parties."

"Well, that sounds like personal responsibility if I've ever heard it." Dark eyebrows dashing up, he tugged at my laptop screen. "What are you studying vocab for? A test or something?"

"A paper. Why?"

He shrugged. "Just figured I might be able to help. You know, since it's my fault?"

Well, that was rich. The big, dumb rich boy trying to help me. "And what would you know about psychology terms?"

Over my shoulder, he tugged up my failed psych quiz from under my computer, smiling again. "A lot more than you. Yikes—"

I ripped the quiz away. "I don't need your help, and I'm sure Haley's missing you."

His smile left as he stared at me, his big arms folding over his chest. "I was actually helping Haley with one of her computer classes. Was pretty into that stuff in high school."

"Yeah?" I turned, staring right at him. "Was that before or after you fucked her?"

Eyes darkened right away, a pulse shooting straight into my chest when he reached around me and grabbed my computer.

"Hey!"

He snapped it shut, forcing it into my computer bag before shoving my books and papers inside along with it. "Put some shoes on. We're going somewhere."

Like hell. I reached for my bag, but with his size, he easily dashed it beyond my grab. He tucked the bag over his shoulder, then with a fist full of my hair, he made me look up at him. "I'm going to show you I know a fuck of a lot more about all this shit than you. Now, put your damn shoes on. I'm going to help you with your psych shit whether you want it or not."

He let go, completely serious, and the only reason I slipped my shoes on and followed behind him was because I was afraid he'd pick me up and throw me over his shoulder if

I didn't. I closed the dorm, locking it behind us. "Where are we going?"

"You'll see," he said, texting Haley in the hall. I saw her name across the screen and again, tried to ignore how I felt about the fact that he was obviously letting her know what he was doing. That she maybe meant something to him. I backed up when he looked at me. His eyes narrowed. "I'm parked outside. We're going for a drive, and I hope you don't have anything else to do today. It'll take us a while to get where we're going. About two hours or so."

What the fuck?

I kept up, but couldn't mask my fear. This guy had been known for his crazy before, and here I was going along with it. I didn't know what that made me, but probably just as obsessed with him as Haley and the rest of my roomies. What else could explain that I was doing exactly what he wanted me to do?

I just hoped I didn't regret it.

CHAPTER
ELEVEN

Greer

"I didn't fuck Haley by the way." Knight lounged in his seat, his hand roving the Escalade steering wheel. His eyes glanced over. "You know, in case you were wondering?"

Since I wasn't, I adjusted in my seat, clamped the hell up with my book bag in my arms. I hadn't even put it on the floor, my stuff and purse still on my lap.

"You can relax." For emphasis, he took my stuff, shoving it in the back, and it took all I had not to punch him right in his face. He was so aggressive, all that completely unnecessary.

I shoved my arms over my chest. "Where are we going?" We'd been driving for over an hour of his two-hour drive, silence between us besides the hip hop he had playing in the car. This was instrumental, unlike the last he'd played, smooth and easy listening beats.

"Maywood Heights," he said, and when I shot back in my chair, he rolled his eyes. "The place I'm taking you to is there."

"What place?"

He shot me a look. "Just relax. We're going to be there soon enough, and then you'll see."

Then I'd see, the place and town he'd run my mom and me out of the first time. His grandpa had been furious about that whole dog thing, thought, even at nine years old, I could create problems for Knight and his family if I told someone. The whole thing had been ridiculous. I'd been more scared if anything, more scared of Knight. The last thing I'd been thinking about was running my mouth and ruining whatever reputation his grandpa wanted to upkeep about his crazy grandson. That was the Reeds, though, maintaining the status quo nothing if not important.

I could see that now, probably the reason Knight wanted me to keep my mouth shut about that night with Bryce in the first place. He didn't want me making noise about whatever happened that night, tarnishing who he was.

I simmered inside next to him, *trying* not to look at him as he navigated the road and especially in the moments when our gazes actually clashed and mine wanted to hold on, look deep into those brown-black eyes and see his secrets. They were secrets that definitely didn't serve me, but I couldn't help but want to know more. There was so much mystery about him, so much darkness and sin. I wanted to know where it came from, how someone at the age of eleven could have even been capable of doing what he had. He was seriously screwed up and a lot of that translated now.

I mean, he'd taken me captive again.

I swallowed staring at the road when eventually, we did pull up to that Maywood Heights' welcome sign. A seemingly happy town, the small city was nothing but modern age with a rural fare. There was something small and quaint about the Midwestern city, but it was expansive enough to show quite a few people lived their lives there. Since it was

Saturday, the roads were busier than normal with shoppers and traffic, but Knight easily worked his way through. His Escalade was an eyesore amongst the hatchbacks and mini-vans, but there were quite a few luxury cars definitely peppered in there too, the elite amongst the common folks.

That's how I felt in this car with Knight, his arm out the window as he drove. Eventually, we cut away from the main part of town and to some of the back roads, and that's when Knight told me to prepare for where we were coming up to.

Maywood Heights Communities, the sign said, and Knight pulled up to a gated entry. After speaking with the guard, they let him in, and Knight took the path down to a large brick building that looked like a hospital, people being assisted as they crossed the roads in wheelchairs. I didn't understand why he brought me here, nor why we were here.

Knight's Escalade took up a parking spot and a half and shutting off the truck, he reached for my things, returning them to me.

"Can I be let in on what's going on now?" I asked, getting my bag on my arm. I'd shoved my purse inside, getting out when he did.

Knight came around, his hands in his pockets. "We're here to help you with your psych stuff."

"And *here* would be?"

"A nursing home," he said, his voice serious as he backed up. "And try to keep up?"

A… nursing home? Well, that made sense now with all the people in wheelchairs and stuff. There were also people in scrubs helping to mill them around, and I picked up my feet, not keeping up easily with Knight and his long strides. He took one for like my three, and I nearly fell into him when he stopped at the door.

He secured me with firm hands, righting me. "You good?"

"Erm, yeah." I backed away, backed *off him*. He dropped a

hand to his side, and with a lift of the eyes, he was pulling open the door. I shoved my way quickly past, then let him take the lead as we walked up to a sign-in desk with a woman in scrubs behind it.

"Knight Reed. Is that you?" the woman behind the desk asked, a large grin on her face.

Knight had a bit of a smile as we walked up to the desk, his hands returned to his pockets. "Yeah, Janet. It's been awhile. How are things?"

"Good, honey. Good. And yeah, it has been a while. Good to see you, though." The nurse's gaze moved around his mass to me. They lit up. "You bring a friend today?"

I didn't know about all that, but Knight did nod before he was handed the sign-in sheet. He signed his name, then handed it over to me.

"How is she today?" he asked while I signed, and looking up, I noticed the woman's expression change, her eyes a little sad.

"Always the same, sweetie," she said, folding her hands. "But you're welcome to see her as always. I'm sure it'd help to hear your voice."

His… *voice*.

Knight said nothing, nodding at her before stepping away from me. The woman smiled super wide at me after that, and so confused about everything, I just smiled back since she was being kind. I truly had no idea what was going on here, but Knight definitely seemed to know this place. A few people acknowledged him along the way, both hospital staff and not. Patients knew him too, ones playing chess and others being wheeled around. These people knew him, and though he wasn't much for words he knew them too, always passing them a few words in greeting before going about his way.

I kept up. "Knight…"

He turned as he pressed an elevator button, the frown hard on his face. "For once, can you *not* with yourself today?" The elevator door pinged open, and we both stepped inside. He tapped a button with his fist, then scrubbed in his dark hair. "Just not here. Not today."

His gaze parted from mine, and I was truly left without words, the elevator ride as quick as it started. It pinged open again, and I followed his heavy strides down a hall not as active as downstairs, medicinal tones in the air. Downstairs definitely felt more like a nursing home with all the patients, but up here, a hospital through and through. I kept up as best I could, and when we got outside of the door, Knight stopped.

His eyes narrowed. "I just ask that you don't be rude, okay?"

Why would I be rude? And who did he know here? He opened a door, and the sunlight from the room flooded in, a huge bed with a woman in the center of it.

I came inside and I saw her, raven-black hair down to her shoulders and with her eyes shut. They had her hooked up to all kinds of IVs, machines that pinged and beeped like she was some kind of science experiment. I followed Knight over to her bedside, and completely in her space, I was awed.

She was strikingly beautiful, like something in catalogs or on the silver screen. Her skin pale and features soft, the light in the room only brought out more of her beauty, and when I truly looked at her, she looked so familiar to me it wasn't even funny. I'd seen her before.

Or at least her face.

It was so similar to Knight's, soft where he was hard edged. This was especially noticeable when he came around the bed, hovered above her. He touched her face, his knuckles brushing her cheek.

"Knight?" I questioned, watching him watch her. The woman didn't even move at being touched, no shift or jump or anything. She merely lay there, and when Knight sat down at her beside, the same. His eyes came up to meet mine, his expression hard and completely cold.

"This is my mother," he said, and the gasp left my throat. "And as you can see she's in a coma."

CHAPTER
TWELVE

Greer

A coma… no way, but not only was Knight serious, but dead serious. He stared upon the woman, his hand cupping her shoulder. His touch swallowed her whole shoulder, that's how small she was and big he was in comparison.

I shrunk slowly to a seat beside the bed, not wanting to make too much noise. I thought, illogically, that any sudden movements might shatter something. I dampened my lips. "What happened?"

He had… a mom? I mean, of course he had a mom. We all had one, but I never knew of his. When my mom and me had been living at his grandpa's, it'd been just him and Knight, no one else. I assumed, as a child, I'd guessed something had happened to them, but I'd been so young I never bothered asking.

Knight's knuckles brushed his mom's shoulder this time, the breath easing heavy from his lungs. "She was in a car accident." He sat back, his eyebrows narrowing. "Happened when I was real young. Before you and your mom came to live with Grandfather and me."

That was well over ten years ago. I lowered my bag to the floor. "How long has she been in a coma?"

Dark lashes shifted left. "Twelve years."

Holy fuck.

That was like half his life. My God, and looking up, I swallowed. "You were nine?"

"Yeah, the whole thing was not long after my dad died. He was in a riding accident mere months before it happened. It was fucked."

Jesus. I faced the woman, her appearance nothing but a pleasant sleep. If you didn't know, you wouldn't *know*, and Knight, he didn't even look sad, more so used to all this. And maybe he was.

Half his life….

"It was a traumatic brain injury that put her in the coma," he said, looking over at me. "Sound familiar with your class stuff?"

It did, one of my psych terms because of its connection to mental impairments. I wet my lips. "Do they think she'll ever come out of it?"

I felt stupid the moment I said it, like putting that reality out there might make things worse for him instead of helping, and now, I knew why he told me not to be rude outside the room. This was a sensitive issue here, all this *very sensitive* and extremely personal. For whatever reason, he shared that with me and I didn't understand.

He crossed his legs at the knee, mighty hands resting on his boot. "I used to wish for a long time she would." He shook his head. "Wished it with all I had."

His voice rough on the end, something pulsed inside of me, my heart.

He wet his lips. "I barely even remember who she used to be now. Grandfather had her moved here, keeps her comfortable for me." He shrugged. "He obviously only does it for me."

"What's the alternative?"

"Stopping all this." He raised his hand to the machines. "Taking her off life support. If she hasn't come out of it by now…"

He said the words so final, so unfeeling. It was like he'd played this conversation so many times already in his head, merely vocalizing it now.

Maybe he had.

"Sometimes, I wonder if it'd be easier," he said, glancing away from her and up at me. "If anything for her. It's like she's just here in limbo, no way forward or back."

But at least *this* gave him hope, at least a little bit? Right? I leaned forward. "I don't know if it's that simple."

His eyes cut to me, cold again. "Because you know so much more about this stuff than me?"

No, but I was trying to sympathize, *empathize* with him? He acted so harsh and jagged sometimes, like a piece of broken glass who's sole purpose was to cut and stab. That was how he'd been treating me, throwing his weight around and watching the world crumble around. It was obviously how he dealt with certain things in his life.

I guessed it was all just really sad.

I had nothing for him now and wished our argument and current situation hadn't made him feel the need to bring me here, to prove a point to me, which was obviously the intent. He did know something about these things, hell maybe even about many of the topics I went over in class about the brain and its relation to mental handicaps. He obviously was a frequent flier around these parts, heard all kinds of stories from doctors and even from the patients themselves by being behind these walls for so many years. This was a nursing home and there were a lot of patients here who needed care, not just in the physical sense.

Knight's hand left his mom again, his Adam's apple working in his throat. "Anyway, it is what is," he said, getting up. He frowned. "And as you could probably see when we came in, there's plenty of people you can talk to about this stuff. Doctors and nurses? They're usually pretty cool about that."

Hence proving my point about what *he knew* about this stuff. He'd obviously been coming here a lot too, talked to many doctors and nurses. A tap at the door, and the woman at front desk came inside the room, her smile wide. "Knight? Some of the other patients and nurses want to say hi. You know, since you haven't been here for a while?"

That saddened me as he looked at her, his nod firm. He started to follow, but shot a glance back at me.

"I'll be fine," I said, getting out some of my school things. "I'll probably do what you said. Get up and find some of those doctors to talk to."

His eyebrows narrowed. "Keep your phone close. I don't want to have to look for you when I'm done."

I told him I would before he left, and though I meant to get up and walk the ward, I couldn't help staring at his mom for a little while. The whole situation was just so sad and I couldn't even imagine.

Her machines hummed around me, and getting up, I did start to leave before noticing one of her charts tucked in a pocket beside the bed. None of that definitely was any of my business, but I did pull it out, take a glance. Her name was Evangeline.

I smiled at that, pulling it out more. They had her diagnosis and a list of all the stuff the her doctors had her on. I assumed fluids and all other kinds of stuff that went well beyond my head. I snapped a picture, not really knowing if I'd need it for anything regarding my paper, but figured it couldn't hurt for perspective when going over my own stuff for class. After, I left everything but my purse and a notebook behind, intending to speak to those doctors like Knight had advised me to do. I bet I could got a lot of information here about both physical and mental diagnoses and decided since I was here, that's what I'd do.

I started to close the door to Evangeline's room before looking at her one more time. I hoped for the best for the situation, but even if his mom did wake up, who knew how she'd be? The whole thing was just terribly sad, but I'd be lying if I said it didn't make a thing or two make sense, a thing or two about Knight?

I closed the door, nothing more I could do.

CHAPTER
THIRTEEN

Knight

I pulled Greer up to her dorm later than anticipated. Fuck, I shouldn't have even taken her to see my mom at all, but she'd pissed me off with all that shit she liked to talk about me being an idiot. I didn't flash my school shit around, but that didn't mean I didn't know anything. Sure, I could take school more seriously, but who couldn't? Didn't mean I was a fucking idiot. Turning off my truck, I reached in the back to get her stuff. She actually put it back there herself this time instead of hugging it for the better part of two hours.

"Thanks." Sitting by the door, she cradled her things, dead fucking silent since we'd left the nursing home. I'd drown some of it out with stuff I'd played though the speakers with my phone, but she'd kept that mouth of hers completely quiet since we left campus. Normally, I wouldn't complain…

But considering recent circumstances.

I had no idea why I'd taken her to see my mom. Hell, *I* hadn't seen my mom at least all term. That shit was hard enough on my best day, still was.

I tapped the steering wheel. "You get everything you need today?" I hadn't stalked her, but did notice she took my advice and talked to some of the medical staff. They had all kinds of information she could use, most of which went well beyond a general education psych class, but I was sure would be helpful for her. I'd personally get more out of talking to an actual psychologist or medical doctor than studying shit in a book, but maybe that was me.

"Yeah, it was really helpful." She played one of her petite, little fingers against the strap of her bag, filling my damn truck up with her little dove scent. She smelled like raspberries and vanilla, and I only knew because I'd been close enough to taste.

I tasted that shit now, trying not to. I unlocked her door. "Good. Glad you got something out of it."

And now she could get out of my truck, no doubt happy to be rid of me for at least a night. My whole life wasn't this girl despite how I was sure it came across to her most days. I had shit to do tonight, my life to reevaluate. I felt really guilty that I'd let so much time pass since seeing my mom, my buddy Royal right. She was around, and with what Janet said about my voice maybe actually helping? I mean, I wasn't naive to believe much of that shit anymore, but it was the least I could do. I loved my mom, missed her.

My hand curled on the wheel, pulling her out of the hospital and moving her to a nursing home the hardest thing. The decision had been up to my grandpa at the time since I'd been a minor, but I could have gotten her out a while ago. I just hadn't known what else I could do for her, and since I was away at school, not much. I'd just been happy Grandfather took care of all that, those decisions so long ago. He still continued to make decisions regarding her care now, and I was happy about that too. I was way too close to the issue, not sure I could do right by her. The easiest thing was letting Gramps do his thing.

Greer wet her lips. "Knight?"

And she was still here, my body lounging back and angling in her direction.

She shrugged. "I'm just wondering why you took me to see her."

I'd told her why, to help her. I shrugged this time. "You said you failing and shit was my fault. Figured I'd be nice."

"But why?"

Why?

I was about two seconds from tossing Greer and that mouth of hers out, but she saved me from that when she finally opened the door. I could breathe a little more when she finally did, no more of that sweet dove scent in my lungs.

She stood at the door. "Thanks. I'm sure it'll be really helpful."

And that's all I wanted, not really knowing why. My hand fisted that steering wheel until she finally closed the door, and with a start, I was peeling out of that lot quicker than the day I'd originally dropped her at her dorm. Honestly, I didn't know why I'd taken her to see my mom.

Honestly, it was stupid.

The frat was gratefully silent by the time I made it back that night, and sitting outside, I took a moment before heading in. I didn't know why, some fresh air good for my head. I left the windows down and sat back, and fuck if I knew how long I'd actually sat out there before coming inside. I opened the door and got a few handshakes from a couple buddies inside, but not two seconds in was I told I had a visitor.

He'd been waiting for me, I guess.

Grandfather stood inside my room when I made it there, hand on his cane as he stared at a personal photo.

"I called you, son," he said, truly this man's son. He was basically the only father I ever had. I'd been a child when I lost Dad, his memory fading as well. I admit I hadn't checked my phone today, with Greer all day.

I closed the door, coming over to my grandpa. He held a family photo of my mom, my dad, and me, his hand firm on the frame.

"I remember taking this photo of your guys," he said, tilting his head at the family photo in the mountains. We all stood at the top of a rock. "Remember it?"

I did, though it was so long ago. We'd all gone hiking, no one to take a photo of us all out there. It'd been Grandfather to step up and take one of my parents and me, always the one sacrificing. Gramps handed it to me, and I smiled a little upon holding it. "I do. It was a fun day."

"It was very nice."

I nodded, setting the photo down. "Didn't know you called. Sorry. I've been out all day."

"Mhm, I know that." He took a seat on my armchair, gesturing for me to do the same. I had a matching set across from my personal fireplace, most of these rooms did. Gramps's head tilted behind his mustache. "I got a call from Dr. Silvera today. He said you went by to see your mom?"

I frowned, Dr. Silvera my mom's main doctor. "He did? Why?"

My grandpa tilted his head back and forth. "I'm always in talks with him about your mom's care. Since the nursing home hadn't seen you in a while, he just thought to inform me. Found it curious."

It shouldn't be. I shrugged. "She's mom."

"Yes, son, but you haven't made much of an effort to see her lately." Because he was right, I said nothing. He frowned. "Any particular reason today?"

I obviously couldn't tell him about Greer. He shouldn't know about Greer *at all* considering she'd been here that night with Bryce, and though this scenario had no relation to that one, I didn't want to take the chance. "No, sir. Just went to see her. Like you said, it's been a while."

Grandfather's hand moved over his cane, his eyes sad. "I've actually been talking with her doctors more and more recently. You know she's unchanged."

I did, nodding. My mom's prognosis hadn't changed in the years since she'd been in the dark, no hope, at least told to me anyway, that anything *would* change. It'd been something I'd long accepted a while ago. But still, her being my mom, I'd never wanted to give up hope, still didn't.

Grandfather reached over, gripping my shoulder with the hand that shined his own Court ring. He squeezed. "I think you're of the age to make the decision yourself, but you might want to start considering what's next for her. You're twenty-one now and… those decisions need to be made."

I knew that, knew that ultimately it would be me to call it. But still, even thinking about it…

The thing whole made my stomach sick, my head shaking, and Grandfather squeezed my shoulder again.

"I won't pressure you," he said. "Never would. I just want what's best for you. Best for her too. She was married to my son, and I've always loved her."

He had, all of us really close. I nodded. "Can I think about it?"

"Of course," he pulled back, this discussion hopefully over now, and I was grateful when I later escorted him back downstairs. As it turned out, since he couldn't get a hold of me, he'd decided to come over, check on me personally after hearing I'd seen Mom today and I appreciated that.

"Be sure to let me know if you ever come to town again? To see her?" he asked by the door. He smiled at me. "I'll always go with you. You know that."

And I'd needed that for sure way back when, those early days when I'd been a fucking mess and couldn't see the world right. I'd wanted to destroy *everything* in sight, so angry.

I nodded again, opening the door and started to walk him outside before we both had to stop. Someone else was on the other side of the door.

And she looked scared to hell.

Greer

I'd been in my dorm room about two seconds before I realized I'd left my notebook in Knight's car. I guessed I could have called him about it and probably should have.

I supposed I had just wanted to check on him.

I didn't know why really and for whatever reason, I found myself in a ride share instead of picking up my phone and texting him. I *should have* texted him, texted him for many reasons and the main one being the look he gave me the moment the door blew open and spotted me in front of it. His expression transformed into one of the wild, an unfurled anger of increased intensity the longer he stared at me. He left the door in an instant, a man standing behind in the distance. I was unable to see him long because Knight had me by the arm, dragging me off the frat house steps and down the way I came.

"What the *hell* are you doing here?" Like stated, wild the way he stared at me. His expression appeared maddened, completely crazed. He threw me away from him, basically like trash. "What right have you—"

"Son?"

His eyes twitched wide as he turned, that man I could see now. Older, he had a presence and familiarity about him I'd recognized from the past. This man was Gerald Reed.

This man was Knight's grandpa.

The older man stood upon the frat house porch like an emperor, one overseeing his kingdom and the actions before him. He frowned. "Knight, son. Who is this?"

My eyes twitched wide, the man clearly not recognizing me. Though I wasn't surprised. I'd been only a kid the last time he'd seen me, and I had been surprised Knight had even recognized me when I'd been at that party. We'd recognized each other, both of us like lantern to its light. We'd found each other.

I wished we hadn't.

I'd had my reservations about coming here tonight, for *so* many reasons and actually had felt ill on the way over. I had no intention of actually going into the property, being there where Bryce shot himself. I still remembered his face, all that blood, and Knight's face in return. I'd never seen him scared before and hadn't since, absolute terror in his eyes at what had happened in front of us both. He hadn't had the look of a guilty man, only a part of that sole action being taken by another. He'd been shocked, fearful, which had been all the more reason I'd been confused why he'd taken me out of there. He clearly hadn't wanted what Bryce had done to happen. But for whatever reason he was *making* himself guilty of something by pulling us away. It'd been wrong. It'd been weird.

I swallowed, starting to open my mouth and address his grandpa. I was going to reintroduce myself, share who I was with him since technically, we had known each other at one time.

"She's no one, Grandfather."

Right in the chest as he cut in front of me and then forgotten as he graced the steps, standing by his grandpa. He turned to me, basically sneering. "You know how these girls are."

These… girls?

Another cut at me, another time in which he basically called me a slut and right in front of his grandpa.

My eyes watering, I backed off but not before his grandpa addressed me again, came down the steps to me. Knight stood in the distance this time, his eyes wide but incredibly cold.

His grandpa frowned. "You should probably be on your way, young lady. It's very late."

Very late indeed.

I choked down a lump again as he passed me, Knight not far behind. He grabbed my arm, his hold pinching me. "Get the fuck out of here before I *make* you."

He let go as quickly as he grabbed, heading off behind his grandpa who had a waiting car outside. The engine ran, another man opening the door for him. My ride-share had left but I started to walk in the other direction. I'd find my way back home, damned if I made the same mistake of getting lost again.

CHAPTER
FOURTEEN

Greer

A few short taps and my roommates appeared in my room. They looked amazing. Sophie with her hair all done up and dressed to the nines, and Keisha in a baby blue dress that highlighted the varied tones of her voluminous curls. The kicker had been Hales, her pink dress short, petite and making her look too cute. These girls were dressed for clubbing and not only that.

"We're kidnapping you," Haley said, then from behind her back she pulled out the most exquisite glistening dress. Powder white, the dress looked like literal sparkles and sequins and was short enough if I bent wrong I'd have a major vagina slip.

I frowned, shaking my head before going back to my books. "I need to study, sorry."

Something they could take note of, and how the tides had turned. I hadn't seen them all in days, a far cry different from the previous week. I only didn't complain because that meant I *hadn't* seen Knight and his crazier-than-fuck attitude since that day he'd kicked me off the frat's property. I was completely over it, *over him*, and still hadn't gotten my notebook back. I took a few notes on my phone from the nursing home so at least that'd been helping when I started my paper.

All three of the girls shimmied into my room, making me groan when they pulled me to my feet.

"This isn't an option." Hales framed my body with the dress. "We're going to do your hair, then you're going out. You've been studying way too much."

Again how the tides had turned, my messy bun ripped down, then fluffed out. With a tug, they got my hoodie off, but when they went for my bed shorts, a now permanent fixture in my wardrobe as of late, I drew the line. I ripped the dress from Hales. "Thanks. I can dress myself."

Snickering, they all shook me before I scooted them out of the room and took a look at this dress they'd managed to round up for me. Seriously, half the club would be looking at my goods tonight, but maybe that wouldn't be a bad thing.

At least, Knight wouldn't be there.

He wasn't here now so they obviously hadn't invited him and his crew to come along, and what if they were? I was a free woman and could do whatever the fuck I wanted. *Especially* when it came to him.

I took the moments to get dressed, taking extra care with my hair and make up before putting my best fuck-me pumps on, then scooted out the door with my friends. Hales was the only one of us who had brought a car to college, so we took it and headed downtown to the best underage club. They allowed all ages there, of course, but this was the best one we could get into and was where I'd actually met Bryce that night.

Swallowing at the memory of that, I opened my purse, swiping my lips with an extra coat of gloss before heading inside with my friends. Keisha got us right up to the bouncer and with a few words was able to get us in front of the line and right inside. She was good like that, despite being such a nerd like all my roommates were. She was a smart and beautiful nerd like the rest of them, all three of them easily getting what they wanted if they cared about such things. Funny enough, I wasn't the one who fit in now, more so keeping to myself. A few evenings in with Knight and his lot and my friends were tossing all inhibition, being bold, and we were noticed the minute the strobe lights hit our eyes.

Guys circled us left and right, but we danced together, Hales tugging my hand while the others danced around and beside us. I was a bit stiff, but with some probing they got me to let go and laugh a little, tugging my arms and making me dance. Spinning, I danced around Sophie, grabbing Keisha in too, and it was so much fun to just let loose and be a freshman again. I'd started the year so carefree, so different now, and I hated that.

"Oh, gosh. It's Knight!"

Absolute dread as Hales tugged my arm to face that direction, Knight and his crew in VIP. They all sat at a high-top table, gratefully *across* the room, with Knight in the center of the group. A king in his castle, Knight had a girl I recognized under his arm, Melrose he'd introduced to me that night at the frat.

I idly wondered if they were fucking, but since none of that mattered to me anymore, I took Haley's hand and danced with her. She frowned. "You don't wanna say hi?"

I could imagine she had more of a relationship with him than I had. After all, he had been helping her with her homework that day. Honestly, I thought he'd been bullshitting me, the guy an obviously complete manwhore. He had women dripping off him all the time and had the audacity to say the shit he had about me.

"I'm okay," I told her, then frowned myself. "But you're free to."

He hadn't seen any of us yet, his attention divided with

his arm wrapped around another girl. Currently, *said girl* nuzzled his neck, that arrogant grin on his face as he drew off a beer. His buddies clinked their own bottles as they congregated around him, with their own girls and own set of privilege. The entire display caused me to roll my eyes, and though Haley looked a little deflated to see him busy, she had come back to me.

"Maybe later," she said, then cupped her hand around my ear. "Wanna get some drinks?"

I wasn't thirsty quite yet, but since she and the others appeared to be when they came over too, I told them they could go. I was, on the other hand, in need of a good freshening up already, so I decided to do that while they went to the bar. I think I was in the bathroom for all of a second before I was ready to come back out, a girl's face over the toilet. She ralphed her lungs out to kingdom come, so after a quick fluff of my hair, I was right back out on the dance floor. I didn't see my friends right away so I decided to head to the bar.

"Can I get you something?"

The bartender yelled for my attention and waving him off, I rested my elbows back on the bar. I spotted Keisha and Sophie out there, drinks in their hands. I waved to them for their attention, but they weren't seeing me, deep in the pit. I started to go that way too before I found Hales. She was in the pit, but she wasn't with them.

Knight had her, by the hand as she spoke to him. He was no longer in VIP, a towering mountain in his denim jeans and dark jacket. He was obviously fluid with that girl Melrose because he now loomed largely above my roommate, grinning at something she said, and when his eyes lifted, I froze.

He stared at me, stared at me full on while he brought my roommate into a dance. Before, he'd just been talking to her, but at the present, dancing seemed to be his main priority when he took her close and grabbed her hips. She fell into him easily, of course, tucking her little body up against him, and with a spin, he had her ass against his crotch, his long wingspan falling around her. He enveloped her, hugging her close with a simmer in his eyes only reserved for me.

I burned as I watched him, the fury matching what I had before the evening he'd once again embarrassed me. He'd done that right in front of his grandpa, making it even worse and twisting the dagger in a way only he could. He knew how to hurt me and the exact ways in which to do it. The only difference between us was I'd never been able to figure out how to gain the upper hand. Outside side of my "mouth" as he said, I merely annoyed him.

His fingers laced with Haley's, when his nose brushed her neck, I'd had enough. I turned to the bar, steaming, and when I got the attention of a guy holding a beer, I smiled at him.

He smiled right back at me, a nice looking guy, blond with blue eyes. He raised his beer to me and tapping the bar, I came over to him.

His grin widened. "Can I buy you a drink?"

My eyes shifted to the dance floor, but not long before I was taking the man's beer and sucking it back. His eyes twitched wide as I downed his drink, that shit strong and foul tasting as fuck since I didn't really drink. I mean, I was underage and usually only had like wine coolers at parties.

Chuckling, the guy touched the bar for another beer, and once he got it, he clinked to me. "You want something else?"

I wanted to dance and work off all this restless energy, and when I put the empty bottle on the counter, I tugged at his shirt. "How about we dance?"

He readily accepted the offer, *a guy*, and after getting a few good swallows of his beer, he threw an entirely too heavy arm around me and guided us off to the dance floor. I made sure we were right in the center, right in the middle of the action, and though I'd lost sight of my friends, lost sight of *Knight* and my friend I didn't care. Something told me he would be watching.

He always did.

This guy grabbed my hands, raising them up before tucking me into his side. He put a hand on my hip, grinding on my ass, and I didn't particularly fancy that but didn't tell him to stop. He hugged me to him close, pulling me in front of him by the hips, and I ground my own ass into him, his package instantly getting hard. He formed his hands around my hips, but only just touched them before he let go, his heat backing off me. Since it came close right back, I closed my eyes as his hands drifted down my hips.

He hugged them, hugged them tight as he pushed himself up against me again. Tones of peppermint and warm heat drifted off him, twisting my tummy up as all that reminded me of someone else.

Behind my own lids, I envisioned that someone else, his hands and big arms coming around me, holding me close. The guy behind me brushed his nose against my ear, his teeth skidding, then tugging my earlobe into his mouth.

"What are you doing, little dove?"

I froze, the hands in front of me doing the same, going tighter as they braced me to a hard body. My eyes fell open. "Knight…"

He said nothing, though I knew it was him, his hands swaying my body. So hard, he tucked his cock right between my ass cheeks, and I simmered, swallowing hard. He pressed a hand right against my mound, forcing my ass into him more. "I know what game you're playing, dove, and it won't work."

"What game?"

"This?" His knuckles dragged across my shoulder, his finger hooking my sequin strap and pulling it down. He breathed heat over it. "Trying to make me jealous."

But the fact that he'd noticed let me know he was, the fact that another guy had been dancing with me but suddenly wasn't even more. I had made him jealous. I'd played his game and won.

So why was I the one melting under his hands? Why was I the one burning as his teeth pinched at my dress strap? This game was turning dirty, the devil's dark corruption.

I wanted to tell him to stop, to scream at him and punch him right in his gorgeous face for all the cruel and evil ways he'd tortured me in the past. I wanted to hurt him, not turn him on, which clearly this all was.

His mighty arms enveloped my body as he'd done with Hales before, and even though I had no idea where she was now, his attention obviously had never been there. He'd been trying to make *me* jealous, it definitely working.

"So now what are we going to do about it?" His hand covered my throat, squeezing and making my pussy lips burn. His chuckle was thick. "Because if I had my way I'd be deep inside you right now for trying to mess with me."

I shuddered imagining that, and instinctually, my ass hugged his dick. It froze *him* this time, his other hand guiding my hip away.

"Dangerous, dove," he warned, so much grit and arousal in his voice. He groaned. "You don't wanna know what will happen if you keep doing that."

I did it again, pushing back his hand and making him brush against me. He grunted in my ear, the heat completely simmering off him.

"One more time," he threatened again, his hands reaching and gripping both my wrists. "Don't test me."

So serious, I turned back to look him in the eyes. The madness there teetered that line of control, his dark hair curling wildly over his eyes. This was probably incredibly stupid and definitely foolish, but I also know he wouldn't see it coming.

I hadn't until my lips met his.

He stiffened again as I sucked his bottom lip into my

mouth, tasted him and made him taste me, and groaning, his hand gripped my cheek, tugging me close and kissing me back.

He couldn't stop once he started, his tongue delving into my mouth, and I didn't want him to stop. I wanted him close.

I wanted him completely.

His hand fell to my neck as our lips parted, and when his grip encased my throat this time, his thumb brushed down my windpipe. "Come back to frat just after three tonight," he said, wetting his lips. "We finish this there."

CHAPTER
FIFTEEN

Greer

I had to have lost my mind because not only had I decided to take a ride share back to the frat house later that night, but I asked Haley about it. She'd not only *not* been surprised by the invite, after all Knight had kissed me on the dance floor, but then asked me what had taken so long. Apparently, both she and the other girls had picked up on some "tension" between Knight and me, but since I'd told her I wasn't with him that day at lunch she'd gone for it.

She'd even apologized if she potentially stepped on my toes.

All of this was so goddamn wrong it wasn't even funny. Knight Reed was a monster. Knight Reed was arrogant, but still, I found myself back at the very place he'd tossed my ass out of not days before. The frat house had been completely quiet at 3 AM, no parties or anything, and I didn't know how I felt about that. I didn't know how I felt about being there at all. I just knew Knight had challenged me again.

And for whatever reason, I wanted to be up to it.

My heart raced as I stood outside on the frat house's porch, the place like a cabin in the woods but mansion-sized. It was beautiful, completely surrounded by nature and wildlife. The guys had their own little abyss out here not far from campus, and the door opened before I could even knock. Knight stood in the door frame, waiting for me in a long sweater and slouchy sweats that cuffed at his ankles, his feet bare on the wood floor. I didn't know when he'd left the club. Maybe way after me. Maybe not, but he'd had enough time to shower. Hair freshly washed, he worked a towel through it, his hair glistening and sleek like a panther's fur when he dropped the towel over his broad shoulders. He grinned. "You didn't stand me up."

More of his games, a clear challenge on that dance floor tonight. He'd wanted me to back down, but it had been me to kiss him. I did it because I wanted to.

I just didn't understand why.

It was him and his draw, *always* this attraction between us. It frightened me and was the reason I was standing here tonight.

Knight widened the door, and though I dipped under it, I kept my personal space.

"Did I have an option?" I asked, turning around, and he pulled the towel off his shoulders. Tossing it on an empty section of the frat's couch, he pinched his fingers out, tugging me closer by the jacket.

"You always have a choice, little dove," he said, easing my jacket off my shoulder. "Now stay awhile."

I breathed harshly as he slid the jacket down my shoulders. Still in my dress from earlier tonight, it glistened even in the low lit room.

"Fuck." His groan heated his eyes, the jacket in his hands only moments. He hooked it on a coat rack before tugging me with him, his hand in mine as he escorted me to the kitchen. We got inside, and he flicked on the light, the kitchen large and easily sized to occupy a dozen men. Since that was the case I was sure most days that made sense.

"You want something to drink?" he asked me, his hand leaving mine. He opened the fridge. "We have soda. Milk?"

I watched him as he chose for me, both options in front of me. I honestly didn't want either, too nervous. I'd never done any of this before, whatever we were doing. I pointed to the two liter and he got something together for me in a clear glass.

"Everyone in bed?" I asked, the place too quiet. Made me even more nervous. Knight returned with a glass of milk for himself, guzzling it down, and the entire display made him all too hot. Especially when he dragged a finger across a slight milk mustache.

He noticed me watching his lips, his perfect mouth as he cleared it from the milk. He smirked. "Whole house is empty. Cleaning crew comes once a month and completely wipes down the place. We all usually stay with friends or some shit until they give us the okay to come back."

Hence, the 3 AM invite.

Holy fuck.

Knight came over to me, and my heart flipped, all of this a mistake. This was going way past games or even beyond the physical. This was deeper, emotional and raw at least on my part. I was feeling something for him. I *felt* something for him as stupid as it may be, and it was stupid. This had to be all just a game for him.

And how fucking good he was at it.

His finger curled, brushing my neck, and my heart basically imploded beneath my rib cage. His hand cuffed my neck, and I knew he could feel my pulse. I *heard* it, so loud and deep in my head. I wet my lips. "What are you going to do?"

An honest question, and I wanted some fucking honesty. I needed to know his intent, if this was all just a game still.

If he wanted to hurt me again.

He could so easily shatter me and rip me a part. It was in that moment I realized how much power he actually had, his finger running along my throat now.

"What do you want me to do?" he asked, my flesh on fire as he dragged his finger down to my chest. He outlined the top of my breasts, my breath in-taking. "You're the one who came here tonight."

Because *he* asked *me.* I sat up. "I don't know."

Fingers played along the top of my dress, that shimmer glistening against his digits. He had me stand up, his finger tipping my chin. "What do you want me to do?" he asked, pulling me close and bunching the back of my dress in his hand. "Do you want me to kiss you? I can do that. Touch you… well, I can fucking do that too. Tell me what you want. Your call."

It'd never been my call. Ever…

But apparently, it was tonight.

I trembled, trying not to fall apart completely in his hands. "Kiss…"

The word was so soft *I* barely heard it, meek and definitely not me.

His smile coy, Knight angled his body, meeting me halfway as he hovered over my lips. "Kiss you? That's what you want?"

He'd heard me, but before I could tell him no and change my mind, his hand grappled the back of my neck. He kissed me, hard and weakened my knees to the point I slammed my hand on the kitchen island, panting around his taste as his tongue probed and tasted mine.

A slow and gritted, "Fuck," fell into my mouth, his lips devouring me whole. His fist wound around my hair, tight and pulling deep at my scalp. I gasped, opening my mouth more for him, and he didn't stop until I couldn't breathe.

His teeth dragged my bottom lip down, his finger

pinching it. "I want you upstairs. In my room. On *my* fucking bed."

The very prospect had me trembling, but not in ways I believed not that long ago. Our entire relationship previous to this moment had been built on nothing but fear and his sick games. It'd never been this, me actually wanting him. No...

Me fucking needing him.

"Where is it?" I found myself asking. I was drenched between my legs.

His eyes heated as he leaned in, his head jerking toward the door. He let me walk but he hovered close, his hands on my hips as he moved me through his house. On the second floor, he opened a bedroom already heated and lit by a fireplace, a beautiful bed with fine silks and drapery all around it. It was lovely and totally *not* Knight.

He closed the door. "Take off your clothes," he commanded, working his sweater over his head. "Now."

I only hesitated at the exposed sight of his chest, a long and muscular body completely perfect to the hipbones. He tossed his sweater away, his pecs jumping with dark nipples. A smattering of dark hair chased a line down to the fastened seam of his jeans, his bulge ready and thick as he passed a hand over it. Waiting, he watched as I reached for the hem of my dress, a playful gleam in his eyes as I exposed skin.

My tummy jumped as I pulled the dress away, not nearly as tanned as him. I spent my days in hoodies and leggings, shaking down to my fingertips. Approaching, Knight grabbed one of wrists, bracing my hip as he bit down on my flesh.

The pain caused me to moan, his hand easing to play between my legs over my panties. "I said all clothes off, Greer."

Burning, I wriggled out of my underwear, well aware of his dark eyes on me. He studied my every move, letting go as I reached around and unsnapped my bra. The soft warmth of the room did nothing to tame how hard my nipples were, pink and pebbled. He tipped his chin. "On my bed."

I crawled center in, barely on it moments before he was undoing his pants and forcing them and his boxers down his legs. He rubbed his cock, fucking steel as he walked himself over to the bed. It sunk down heavily with his weight and his hand launching out, he turned me on my stomach.

"God, I'm going to fuck you so hard, Greer." He breathed hot kisses down my back, his tongue tasting my spine. "And when I'm done I want that mouth choking around my cock."

Oral sex was amongst the laundry list of things I'd never done just like all this. I was completely and one hundred percent a virgin. Well, if masturbation didn't count.

My mouth watered at even the thought of tasting him, scared but in that fear so turned the hell on. Knight's hand made it between my legs as I considered the thought, his fingers playing with me.

He probed in and out. "So ready for me," he growled, two fingers deep up to the knuckles. "So fucking sexy."

I cried out as he strummed my clit like a string, his digits piston-like as they eased in and out of my body.

"Knight," I gasped and his hand encased my throat, his weight heavy on my back. He turned me around with a single hand, kissing me then as his fingers moved to my nipples.

He pinched them, diamond hard and so sensitive. A struggled cry escaped my throat as he took one into his mouth, sucking my breast nearly whole.

"So sweet," he gritted, his eyes laced with lust. He laved one nipple, then the other, pulling it tight between his teeth. "Too fucking sweet, Greer."

He raised my arms above my head, grinding his cock against my inner thigh, and I ached, barely breathing. I didn't want to breathe, the desire to be consumed by him completely maddening. I groaned as his digits probed me, in and out with so much vigor and beyond anything I'd ever done to myself. Not even with my vibrator.

"You're sin for me, you know that?" he stated, reaching into his bedside table. He tore the condom open with his teeth, rolling it down his dick. "I know you'll ruin me if I let you."

Me ruin him? Not possible. He had to be able to be ruined.

And how could I if he'd already ruined me?

His eyes hazed closed as he probed my entrance, forcing himself in and tearing through me. My muscles tightened at the invasion, but so wet and ready it didn't take Knight long to take himself to the hilt.

He groaned, the pain and pleasure causing my body to shake. He gathered my wrists in both hands, his mouth coming down hard on mine as he slapped against my inner thighs.

"Fuck, Greer." He shuddered against me, if not harder than I was against him. He tasted my tongue. "I'll never make it back from you."

I'd never make it back from him, moaning as he grabbed my thigh and wrapped it around his hip. His abs labored as his hips worked, sweat dripping down his pecs and glistening across his upper lip. He was literally sex on legs and he was fucking me.

"Come for me, Greer," he coached. "Spill around me. I want to fucking feel it."

I didn't last long being a virgin, and no sooner had he said the words than I completely fell over the edge, hot fire burning in my core before stiffening over his mighty cock. He continued to fuck me while I rode it out, reaching that same peak himself as his eyes fell back into his head. Grunting, he held me to him, pressed right up against his chest. It was a place that, before tonight, I wasn't sure I wanted to be, but for whatever reason, anxiety hit that I'd have to soon let go, that he'd let go of me.

My body slumped after he finished, but he easily caught me, still holding on as he brought me into his arms. He ended up bringing his blankets around us, and I was surprised. He'd promised some dirty things for my mouth tonight, but not only did he just hold me, he fell asleep.

I went to sleep to the soothing sounds from his chest, hugging up on him. He said there'd be no coming back from me.

I wondered how that'd change in the morning.

CHAPTER
SIXTEEN

Knight

I forced myself to peel away from Greer in the morning, at a
loss as I cleared my bed. I'd had every intention of fucking
her out of my head last night. That was all I wanted. One
strong fuck to get my mind right, then move on...

Not fucking fall for her.

I'd felt every moment I'd been with her, that taste I had
only made it worse. I hadn't gotten her out of my mind, nor
had I done anything close to veer her away. I hadn't broken
her with our power struggle at all.

She wanted me too.

She hadn't even pretended to not want to be with me last
night. She'd given into it, easily and maybe even as badly as
I'd wanted her. It had taken all I had not to bend her over and
shoot my load off inside her when we'd been together that
first time in her room. Well, now that I actually had her, I was
fucking *gone*. She was ruining me, and for some reason, I
didn't want to resist that. Precisely the reason I got up out of

bed and went downstairs to head into the gym. The house empty until at least tomorrow, I wouldn't have to fight anyone over the machines.

I stayed down there in the basement, wearing myself down until at least eight thirty, and by the time I came upstairs to the kitchen to get a drink, I heard water running from somewhere in the house. I followed the sound to the second floor, *my room*, and after opening the door to my personal bathroom, I saw Greer sinking herself into a cloud of bubbles. She'd made herself a bubble bath, her little face twisted up as she dunked herself in, and I propped a shoulder against the door frame, enjoying the view.

Jesus, she was flawless.

Her perfect tits hovered beneath the water, a snatch I knew to be perfect and unshaven even deeper beneath. She spun around in the heat of the bath, trying to get herself comfortable, and the way her white blond hair dripped water down her back, I wanted to twist it up around my first and rail into her from behind. She was fucking beautiful. Like stated, flawless and I cleared my throat.

She jumped right away, spinning back around, and I grinned.

"Sore?" I asked. She'd looked almost achy as she'd gotten herself in, and when she eased back against the tub, the same.

Shrugging, she glanced over my sweaty frame, my tank drenched to my abs, then down to my more than ready cock. I guess he'd gotten a little excited at the flash of her pussy and supple ass as she'd lowered her inside the bath. I kicked away from the wall. "You're sore? We didn't go that hard last night."

I could have taken her harder, filled all her holes clear into the morning, but I thought I'd lose myself. This girl continued to mind-fuck me, last night no exception.

"I wouldn't know," she said before spinning, shy and

meek as she put her back to me. She hugged her legs, staring out the window into the woods, and it took me all of about two seconds to realize what she was talking about. I'd told her we hadn't gone that hard, and she'd said she didn't know another way.

Fuck.

The curse left my lips as I scrubbed into my hair, and she peered over her shoulder at me when I crossed the room. "Move over. I'm getting in."

Her eyes launched wide immediately, so fucking shy now. She covered herself. "I'm really sore."

"I know." I gripped the tub, hunkering down. "I promise no sex. I just going to help you wash."

Had I had any idea this girl hadn't been touched before I wouldn't have nearly been so heavy handed. I mean, we still would have been together but not like that.

A flash of stark white lashes, and I wasn't sure she quite trusted me. I guessed I couldn't blame her. I'd given her more than one reason not to in the past, but in the end, she did move over to the other side of the tub. It was a large tub, had to be to accommodate my ass, and though I didn't take baths often, it was nice after a long work out. The Jacuzzi setting fucking rocked, and I turned it on, making Greer jump a little from the tub walls. I removed my shoes and socks before tugging my shorts down, completely commando underneath.

Greer's little eyes flittered away like she'd *just seen a cock*, and I all out floored myself that I hadn't noticed she was a virgin before. I supposed that night when I fingered her I hadn't really felt any resistance. She'd obviously pleasured herself before because she hadn't been tight last night at all.

I got inside the bath, and only after did she turn herself around, the warmth good on my sore muscles too. I'd worked them to hell downstairs. "Come to me. I'll wash you."

Timid, she eased over, only letting her arms go after she

lowered herself further in the bath. Even with the bubbles I could still see her tits. She frowned. "Why do you want to? You care? You weren't even here when I woke up."

I cared more than she ever knew, this girl so far in my head. "Just let me, okay? I'll go light. It won't hurt."

I knew how to take care of a girl if I need to, make her feel good, and I really wanted to try here. Try here with her.

"You should have told me," I said to her, getting a wash-cloth and sinking it down. I got it nice and drenched before tugging her over to me. "I would have been different with you. More gentle."

Like… this, my hand nudging at her legs until she opened them, *let me* push between them and I did, my touch slick and smooth between her legs. My presence there caused her to gasp, but she didn't pull away. If anything, she wanted me nearer, her hands grabbing my shoulders as I worked the towel gently over and slightly in.

"Feels good?" My voice gruff, my finger escaped and touched her clit. It took all I had not to do anymore.

Her nod was quick, my cock hardening as the rag left my hand and my digits fingered her opening. Greer held onto me for dear life when I did this, and hugging me, she came full onto my lap. A sea of blond hair drowned me as she braced me close and buried her face in my neck.

The rumble rolled in my chest. "You're testing me, Greer."

"Testing you?"

I nodded, letting my finger slide and push back to her ass. Her arms hugged me like her favorite toy, her ass rising above my finger. I grinned. "I take it you've never had your ass played with either?"

"No." The gasp escaped her as she pulled away, staring at me in mock horror.

Chuckling, I removed my fingers from the area and hugged her to me. "Relax. I wouldn't do that unless you were ready. We'd need to open you up a little, use toys?" Her virgin ass would never fit my cock and settling down, she appeared relieved.

"Well, I've never done that. *Any* of that." Her face filled with color, and rolling her eyes, she looked at anything but me. "And why should I have told you? Like you'd have been more gentle."

"I would have," I said, nodding.

"Right. Because you've been so that way before." She escaped me, starting to leave the bath and I tugged her arm. She came back when I pulled her, floating her over onto my lap again.

I folded fingers behind her neck, a perfect flush filling her cheeks. "That's what I said, didn't I? I would have been different. I don't fucking lie." I may have been a lot of things, a brute, an asshole even, but if I said something, I meant it. I curled a knuckle against her cheek. "It's different with you."

Though, I didn't know why. This girl continued to make me do stupid things and even lie to my grandpa about her. I didn't fucking do that, the two of us close, and I'd never felt compelled to before. Gramps and I didn't keep things from each other, but in this case, with Greer involved with that thing with Bryce, I had. It made me question a lot of things, much like this moment now with my hands on her.

Her arms settled around me, staring at me. She played with the hair at the nap of my neck, and I swore to God that shit ran down to my toes.

"Is that why you took me to see your mom?" The words froze my hold around her, pinning me to the tub.

My lips parted. "I told you why. To help with your assignment." She'd said she was failing because of me due to our back and forth. I shouldn't have cared, but I did enough to at least try to help. Her fingers played again with my hair, and I nearly shot my cock into her right there.

Especially when she kissed me.

Her lips came down, hard over my mouth like they had in the club, and she stunned me once again. I was never ready for it. *Ready for her*, but letting her, I turned her, pressing her against the tub. The water sloshed around us, the jets shooting right into her backside, and she bucked, pressing that perfect pussy against me.

"Greer," I growled, cradling the back of her head. "If you don't stop I can't promise no sex in here."

Her only response to that was to rub herself against me, my shit steel and had not a door slammed from inside the house somewhere I definitely would have fucked this girl in my bathtub. The door slam followed stomping sounds a floor below, and freezing, Greer gripped me. "You said no one else would be here."

There shouldn't be, and starting to get up, I came back down at the sound of my name. I recognized the voice.

"He's here. I know he is. His car is here," called December, my buddy's *fiancee* December. "Knight Reed, I know you're here, and you're a complete ass. What's this I hear about you yelling at a girl the other night here at the frat? Get your ass down here and yell at me, why don't you?"

Fucking, fuck. Annoyance that I'd been so fucking candid with who was supposed to be my friend after I yelled Greer off the frat property the other evening. I heard him next, a boisterous chuckle from downstairs.

"Sorry, brother," Royal called a floor down. Another chuckle. "And you better come down here. December's heated up."

"Heated up? Royal, you're supposed to be on my side."

"I am, babe. Calm down. Knight, get down here please!"

At this point, Greer had her hand covering her face, but she must have known this confrontation was about her because she was smiling a little behind her hand. Rolling my eyes, I waded off her.

"Better go," I said, but couldn't help bringing my hand behind her neck and kissing her again. An instant head rush hit right away and something told me this little dove was about to get me in trouble. I'd never done this shit before, all new.

I just hoped whatever this shit was I didn't regret it.

CHAPTER
SEVENTEEN

Greer

Knight came downstairs as summoned, tugging me behind him. I was wearing one of his collared shirts and a pair of boxers because he tossed them at me, and after he stretched a tee over himself and pulled on some shorts we were downstairs, a party at the island in the kitchen. I immediately recognized the couple as his friends from that night with Bryce. The girl, tall and beautiful with hair just as brown-black as Knight's, stood beside another Greek god, the guy's name Royal. He lounged casually against the wall as the girl, December I assumed her name was, flailed her arms at him. She was in a raincoat and rain boots, and Royal smiled at her, more amused by her rant than agitated. I think that only worked her up more if the animation of her limbs and sudden rise of her voice was an indicator. Noticing Knight and me, Royal's attention drifted our way and December's too. She frowned. "Is this her?"

Knight said nothing, but his shrug in her direction let her know what she'd asked was correct. Without warning, she swiped a magazine from the kitchen island and rolled it up. I dodged away as she swung the thing at him, three raps against the chest before a slap at his head.

"December? What the fuck," Knight growled, jerking the thing away from her. This girl was bold because without her paper, she started punching at his arm with her fists. This only amused Knight, his anger leaving completely when this girl clearly wasn't hurting him at all. This only enraged her more, and she launched at him to which Royal finally stepped in and pulled her back by the hips.

"Okay, okay," Royal crooned, tucking her back into his chest. He had to secure her limbs, laughing the whole time. "I think he's learned his lesson, babe."

"Has he?" She reached for him again, but Royal turned her around.

He touched her cheek with a finger. "How about we talk to him? Get his side?"

"What *side*? He yelled at a girl." Her dark eyes fire, she shot a look in my direction. "He yell at you?"

Wanting to stay the fuck out of this, I backed away, all intention of fleeing the room, but Knight neither entertained that or let me. He tucked me behind him, his hand rested softly on my hip as he put out another and attempted to talk this December down.

Standing there, their exchange back and forth, I only watched Knight, *felt* that heat of his hand on my hip. I cradled his bicep, and his attention stole from the conversation entirely.

It shifted to me, his smile a subtle but present one, and I think it took a second for us both to realize December had stopped yelling. We panned together to the other side of the room, and December was doing the funniest thing. *Her* hand was on Royal, all dreamy and doe-eyed as she stared at Knight and me.

Merely chuckling in response, Royal dropped an arm

around December. He leaned into her. "Seems like they worked it out."

I had no idea what we'd worked out. I had no idea what we were fucking doing, but for whatever reason I heated up as Knight laced his fingers with mine. Once there, he tugged me even closer before jerking a chin at Royal."You still good at making omelets?"

"Vegan ones, yeah," December cut in. Chuckling herself, she looped her arms around Royal's waist. "But I guess he's good at the other kind too."

As it turned out the vegan omelets had been for December. I guessed she was a vegan. It was at this point I actually had to admit I wasn't vegetarian because the boys started making up bacon for themselves to go with the eggs, and hell if I was missing out on that.

"Figured," was all Knight said before dashing that sexy-as-fuck smile at me. The presence immediately caused me to stare at his ass when he turned around, his athletic shorts hugging his firm and muscular butt, and noticing me, December waved in Royal's direction. Her eyebrows danced. "Believe me. You'll get used to it."

Her own attention drifted across Royal's backside, and the pair of us laughed, getting more than curious looks from both boys.

December waved her hand again. "Don't worry about us. Please continue."

Royal merely rolled his eyes while Knight stuck his tongue out a little, so playful when he usually wasn't. I liked this side of him, definitely more relaxed. He and Royal continued to make breakfast, and when Royal finished December's vegan omelet with some egg substitute the frat had, Knight plated it, then handed it off to her.

"Vegan omelet for Her Majesty." He bowed to her, his hands together in prayer, and she swiped the magazine again. It lodged straight as his head when she threw it, and growling, he started to take that plate back. "Try that again and—"

"Don't fucking yell at my girl." Royal smacked Knight's arm with the back of his hand, the two bros chuckling. Knight returned December's plate before bouncing eyebrows at me and bending his big body over the counter. "Good, little dove?"

He'd actually made the whole omelet himself, and I nodded, taking another bite. "I suppose it's all right. Could use a little something, though."

"Like class," December finished for me, and I smiled. I think I might like this girl, someone who wasn't afraid to stand up to these big guys.

Knight pointed at her. "Don't fucking teach her things."

"I mean, she's not wrong," I said, agreeing, and his eyebrows launched clear up his face. I smiled. "But then again maybe I like my eggs with a little bit of brute."

I had no idea where that had come from, but I'd been brave enough to say it, tease him. Whatever the case, he didn't hate it, winking at me before going back to the skillet with Royal.

December moved in. "I think you'll fit in just fine," she said. "The trick is to hold your own. If you do, they back off."

"I said don't fucking teach her things." Knight's dark eyebrows descended like storm clouds. "She already has enough of a mouth on her." His eyes softened at me. "But maybe I like a little mouth with *my* eggs."

This exchange caused Royal to shift his body around, shaking his head at the pair of us before dropping his arm around December. Knight said before we came downstairs the pair was engaged, and I pretty much confirmed now it was probably her clothes Knight had given me. He'd called these two for help, to help himself, yeah, but they'd also given something to me.

There was so much about that day that still confused me, but at the moment, I found myself hard-pressed to ask. Things seemed, I don't know, weirdly normal, and Knight didn't scare me like he probably should. That probably had something to do with the fact that Knight couldn't seem to keep either his hands or eyes off me the rest of the morning. I was always in his view, his space, and after eating breakfast, we all reconvened on the couch together. The guys quickly went into playing video games, and though I went to take my own seat, Knight wouldn't let me.

"Here," he said, staking his claim. Keeping me on his lap, he played with his controller around me, tucking me into his bear-sized chest as he yelled at Royal from the other side of the sectional couch. He played too while December watched, her eyes sometimes on the game but mostly on Knight and me. She kept whispering things to Royal too while the boys played, things I couldn't hear, but whatever they were, the conversation had them both smiling. Eventually, Royal played his controller with his arm slung around his girl's waist, and I noticed the ring hanging from her neck. It was a silver one, like Knight's. Currently, Knight wore his, putting it on before we both came downstairs.

"The frat's cleaning crew is going to be here in like an hour," Knight announced eventually, but he didn't stop playing. He continued on against the computer when Royal placed his controller off to the side. Knight grinned. "I assume you'll both see yourselves out."

Royal tossed a pillow at him, calling him, "Fucker," to which Knight returned the same. He'd given Royal an earful for telling December about what happened here while the pair cooked breakfast, and I think the only reason December had let him get away with that was because she'd been talking to me. As it turned out, she went to Pembroke as well, a junior like Knight. Royal was actually a new freshman like me, but the same age. She'd said he'd worked first before going back to school, and they both started this year like I had. She'd transferred in.

December wrestled Knight's hair after getting up from the couch, and after he tossed a pillow at *her*, Royal and December put their coats back on. They'd removed them before breakfast. I guessed it had been raining that morning before they came over.

"It was good meeting you, Greer," December said at the door, smiling at me. She had her hand laced with Royal's. "And don't let that asshole bully you. I just happened to know for a fact he's all bark and no bite once you break him down."

I was starting to see that, but Knight rolled his eyes at what December said. Royal tossed he'd get at him later from the door, and after it closed behind them, I assumed Knight would put the controller down since the cleaning crew was coming. Instead, he only reached over to the other side of the couch. He grabbed Royal's controller, giving it to me. "I thought they'd never fucking leave."

I took it from him, and though I didn't know how to play, I let him teach me. I fucking sucked, first person shooters or really any kind of game not my thing, but eventually, I was able to stick around long enough without Knight immediately sniping me off. Funny enough, I got some good licks in, which hadn't angered him but made him chuckle behind me. It was a nice sound, his laughter, and he didn't do it nearly enough.

"Like this," he instructed, putting down my controller and letting me use his. "You can't run around like a damn squirrel. Stand up for yourself."

My look curious on him, I let him teach me, his hands falling to rest on my hips while he lounged back and let me play. I had to be putting his lap to sleep at this point but he didn't complain.

"Your friends seem nice," I said, passive about it but it

was true. They did seem nice and not crazy like I believed they might be. I mean, they came to his rescue after what happened with Bryce. No questions asked.

"They're all right." He said this, but I definitely heard the smile to his voice. He played with the hem of my shirt, which happened to be his. "Royal asked about how you were doing. And he did remember you from when we were kids once I reminded him."

And how could I forget him? I nodded, the one who held down that dog while Knight crushed its head in. That little blond boy back then seemed like a far cry different from the guy here today. He completely doted over December. But then again, Knight was acting different too.

His hands at my hips while he helped teach me his game, he truly was hot and cold. To the point where it was scary sometimes even. My little man died on the screen, and Knight thought it best we not play anymore since the crew was coming. He put my controller down, but didn't let me go, his hand still full of my thigh. He tapped his ring against my skin, a gorilla's mouth on it.

"I noticed December wore one of these around her neck," I said. He lifted his hand and let me observe it, the thing really scary and so angry. "What is it?"

"Doesn't mean much around here, but it does," he stated, watching me study it. "Half the guys in this frat wear them. It's called a King ring and represents a brotherhood from my hometown. December wears Royal's. He gave it to her when they started dating. As kids, us guys got them in high school, like a fraternity thing but not in college. Doesn't mean as much as it used to. At least to me."

"Why?"

He shrugged. "Because this little ring has made some of the men in my town do some horrible things, power related." He shook his head. "It even got one of my friends killed."

"Jesus." Chills down my arms, Knight's expression terse. He lowered his hand, making a fist with the ring.

"Some dark things have been done due to this ring in the past, but Royal's trying to correct some of them. He's president now, but still, cancer can't always been killed. The Court, that's what we call the society, has bred some truly awful monsters. I come from several generations of the Court. But even our noses aren't clean."

It made me think about that night with Bryce again, so easy the world had been able to move on from that, and I wondered if his boys' club was a part of the reason. The Reeds were very powerful.

I wet my lips. "But you don't have to be like that."

His fingers unfurled, his jaw moving. "I'm *hoping* to be more like my dad. He was Court too before he died, but so *not* Court. At least, how I remembered him. He was a good man. Didn't get caught up in all the shit."

Smiling, I lay against him. "That's nice."

"Yeah. Gramps is a good man too. All this shit's just real hard, you know? Being legacy, a lot of eyes fall on you."

I didn't know, but I did sympathize.

And suddenly the big brute with his privileged past didn't seem so simple. I touched his chest, and Knight pulled back the collar of my shirt, his fingers drifting beneath. "Knight—"

"Stop shaking, dove."

I shuddered instead, his fingers unfastening the shirt's top button before exposing my shoulder.

He tasted with small bites, my skin flushing beneath his teeth. "No one's here. We got a little bit."

He squeezed my breasts through the shirt, and I realized he'd lied to his friends, the cleaning crew coming but obviously not right now.

"No fucking bra," he growled, lowering his head of dark hair. He eased his teeth across my hard nipples, biting and sucking and making the material dark through the shirt.

I moaned, cradling the back of his head as he shifted me off his lap, then on my back. Reaching behind, he tugged his T-shirt off, exposing his hard flesh before balling it up and tossing it on the floor. With a harsh jerk, he pulled at the boxers I wore, sliding both them and my underwear off. Suddenly bare, I forced my thighs together, wriggling. "What if someone comes?"

"No one's coming. I swear to God." He unbuttoned my shirt until I was fully naked, his eyes liquid heat. Touching his mouth down, he dipped his tongue into my belly button. "No one's fucking seeing you but me."

The claim he staked burned my core, that I actually wanted him to exclaim such a thing. That I wanted to be his, completely owned by him as he spread my legs apart.

His eyes darkened at the sight of my already dripping sex, his coal-black locks hanging over his eyes and making him look like a madman. He pulled his thick digits through it, then gripped my thigh, locking it over his bicep. He disappeared between my legs and immediately sucked my lower lips into his mouth.

"Christ. Fuck. Knight."

A chuckle, gravelly and sex-crazed drummed below me, Knight's ridiculously talented mouth doing that again. The third time, his tongue dipped in, the length swiping along my buzzing clit, and my thighs squeezed his head. He forced them apart until I stopped, and I shook, gripping the couch cushions on either side.

"Knight…" I gasped as he entered a digit inside me, quickly moving into drilling me while he tongued me toward orgasm. I was still so sore, but it felt so damn good. I'd never been eaten out at all before, and the sensations were just too much not to give into.

I tried, completely fighting my orgasm. "Knight, stop. Stop! I'm going to come please."

His fingers unfurled from my leg, his laughter subtle as he raised up. "Already?"

I rolled my eyes, starting to push him away but he didn't let me. He nearly took my hand, tugging me up.

"You're cute," he said, kissing me with a smile. "So goddamn sexy."

I was glad *he* liked it, and I forgot about his jab as he kissed me, guiding me back onto his lip. Out of the couch cushions, he pulled a condom and that told me this couch was used for more than just video games.

"How many people have been on this thing?" I asked. Though, I probably shouldn't have. In any sense, the moment Knight tugged his dick out of his shorts a haze hit my brain. The thing was muscled steel, long and hard and pulled up to the first section of his abs.

"Best not to think about it," he said, fisting himself with a hard grip. He frowned at me. "Too sore to do this still or…"

Fascinated with his cock, I think that told him his answer, his smile wide as he ripped the foil wrapper open with his teeth. His eyes simmered. "Wanna help me out?"

He gave me the condom with two fingers and though intimidated, I took it. "What do I do?"

"Just roll it down. Real slow and easy." He leaned back, cradling my hips as he widened his legs beneath me. His breath sucked in the moment I held his dick, his eyes laced with nothing short of lust as I rolled the condom down. "Perfect. Just like that."

So clearly sex drunk, Knight's eyes rolled back, my hand along his steel rod. Knight grunted, urging me to play with his balls, and I did with my other hand. I thought it'd be awkward, but it wasn't, all this so fucking hot.

Knight's eyes opened as he watched me play, his big ole hands coming around my ass cheeks and digging his fingers in. His finger touched my tiny hole, and I gasped. Knight chuckled. "I might play with it while you ride me. Wanna do that?"

He asked me. Needing to know if I *wanted* to do something instead of just doing it and making me. I didn't know what it'd be like if I was with him, but I hadn't imagined this. It felt like he was trying. Like he really was trying to be gentle.

Nodding, I'd like to try what he said, and once told, Knight didn't give me a chance to change my mind. I was still sore, but the moment he lowered me on top of him, pulling me apart I did nothing but moan.

"That's it, dove," he said. Rising up, he dug his teeth into my shoulder, running his tongue along my skin. "I'm going to take care of you."

Shuddering as he moved his hips, I gripped arms around his neck, tucking myself into him and going along for the ride. This felt different than last night having at least done this part before. Different but *good* and with not as much pain as I thought considering I was sore. I opened up for him, riding him.

"Fuck. Fuck. Fuck." He slapped me against the top of his thighs, working himself up and down. His abs and chest glistened with sweat, all that delightful hair leading to his dick. I touched my hands to his perfectly chiseled abdomen, all that power harnessed beneath the skin. He amped up his hips, and that's when he took his fingers to his mouth. He wet his pinky and a couple other digits before reaching behind my ass cheeks.

"Knight. Fuck."

He forced his pinky in to the first knuckle, my bottom surprisingly working against his digit. My fingers scratched at his back, Knight's hips drilling into me as he pushed that digit in more. I felt so full despite him only using his tiniest finger.

"Greer, I'm going to fucking come if you keep making all

these noises," he grunted and pulling out his little finger he headed over another, a longer one, and I stiffened. He smiled. "Relax. I'll go slow."

I tried, falling back onto his finger. I noticed his hips stopped as well but when I moved he moved, like two ships on the same sea. He kept pushing in as I kept working my hips and by the time he got all the way in, my teeth clamped down on his shoulder.

He growled, fucking my ass harder. "If you're going to do it, just *do it*. Bite. Bite me."

We both must have been crazy because for whatever reason, my teeth clamped to the point I tasted him, his skin no doubt red and puckered as I sucked. Knight roared like an animal and fucked me in both holes so hard I actually saw stars as I crested that telltale high.

My body shuddered, my core an intense eruption of heat as I spilled around his cock. A few final slaps of his thighs and Knight was there too, his finger retreating from my ass as he held me close and kissed me full on.

His body slowed as he tasted my tongue and when he peeled my hair away, he framed my face. "Wanna go upstairs? Lie in my bed all day like lazy fuckers?"

The prospect actually danced at my core again, to be wrapped up in him all day. Something was seriously wrong with me, or maybe it was just right? I didn't know, but not only did I tell him yes, I let him carry me up the stairs. He flipped me over his shoulder like a caveman, slapping my ass once we made it into his room, and he kicked the door shut behind us. We literally laid in his bed all day after that. Chillin' mostly and watching TV. It'd been nice.

Being with him had been curiously nice.

CHAPTER
EIGHTEEN

Greer

My psych term paper basically wrote itself after Knight returned my notebook to me, and not only did he give it back, he helped me with it. I wanted his insights, and since I'd included stuff about his mom's condition in there, I wanted to share it with him. He seemed like he not only appreciated it, but wanted to help, truly. I had no idea what was happening here, him and me, but for some reason, I didn't fight it. Things were suddenly very easy with him, where he'd been rigid and abrasive before a thing of the past and I held onto that only too tight. I hadn't wanted to let it go.

I just hoped he didn't either.

I ended up being called to the front one day after psychology class, and since I had just turned in my paper, I was worried a little. Professor Hershel had called me out in the past, and I'd made sure not to sleep in his class since he'd addressed the issue with me. Even still, he stopped me once again when I passed his podium.

"Is there a problem, Professor?" I asked him. He was once

again packing up his things like he had that day he reamed me.

A shake of salt and pepper hair and he was smiling as he finished loading his things. He propped his messenger bag on his shoulder. "I actually just wanted to commend you, Ms. Michaelson. I've started grading term papers, and not only has yours stood out, its leagues above my stack so far."

Shocked, I blinked. "Really?"

"Really." Taking his stuff, he came down off the stage and to the floor with me. "I'm not finished with it yet, but very fine work. I usually don't see such insights in my 110 classes. The topic of mental impairments obviously intrigues you. I only get stuff like this from my graduate students."

Blown away, I couldn't believe what I was hearing. I had tried very hard, and with Knight's help, it'd been cake. He obviously cared about the issue too since I'd included stuff about his mom's condition. "Thank you, Professor."

"No problem. It's still very early, but I have a feeling you're going to do very well not just on the paper but for the duration of the term. I actually had to check the submission was you considering previous discussions we'd had. You've obviously come very far."

I felt I had, definitely not as stressed thanks to a change in the tides. I smiled. "I've been trying to get better sleep."

His eyes warmed. "I'm glad. It would have been a shame not to hear your voice, and it sounds like you definitely have one. The part about traumatic brain injuries was extraordinary and all the other terminology very well researched and insightful. It really sounded like you knew your stuff."

"I tried. I visited a nursing home and got to speak with actual patients with some of the conditions referenced in our textbooks. Their doctors too, so that was helpful."

"Really?" This definitely intrigued him, his smile widening. "Never in my years of teaching have I seen such a display of going the extra mile from one of my freshman students. Especially in one of my gen ed classes. What compelled you to go to a nursing home?"

"I have a friend whose mom is in one. He took me there actually, thought it would help. His mom is in a coma. Twelve years now."

His expression fell. "I'm sorry to hear that. And twelve years? Wow."

"Yeah. She had a car accident, resulted in a TBI, which put her in the coma." He nodded and I continued. "Really heart-breaking."

"I can imagine. I used to practice as a neuropsychologist for many years before teaching. We saw many coma patients, but no one in the condition nearly that long. I'm very intrigued to know more about that. Do you reference it further on in your paper?"

"A little bit, but I only got so many notes when I was at the nursing home. I of course wanted to know more, but since the situation was delicate I didn't pry."

"Makes a lot of sense. Anyway, I just wanted to let you know what a good job you're doing and to keep up the good work. I should have everyone's papers graded very soon. I look forward to finishing yours."

Really appreciating it, I started to walk with him out of class, and when he expressed interest in Knight's mom's case again, I offered to email him over some of the notes I'd drawn up. After I'd lost my notebook, I'd transferred all the information I had gathered from the nursing home on all the patients and doctor interviews over to a Word document and even all the information from the photo I'd taken as well.

Professor Hershel stopped at the door. "Only if you don't mind sharing. I'd definitely liked to see more about that."

Since I hadn't minded, I told him I'd email him every-thing right away. He went about his day, and after I went about mine, I made sure to send him everything over during lunchtime. The day dragged pretty slowly after that, but eventually, I made it to my last class of the day. I'd been struggling in biology just as badly as my other classes, but now that I was awake I'd been able to get some good notes for our test coming up. I came out the room expecting to hop on one of the buses back to my dorm so imagine my surprise when a campus god lounged across the hallway from me.

Knight's thumbs dashed across his phone, wearing a dark leather jacket and jeans that hugged his muscular thighs only too good. He was the epitome of *thicc*, and pulling his hand through his delicious hair, he caught sight of me. A girl or *three* giggled past him as he made his way over to me, and I rolled my eyes. I hadn't expected to see him standing there. He never told me he would be, but then again, when would he ever ask my permission before doing anything at all? He was just rogue like that.

And why did I not mind more and more?

He draped his arm across my shoulders, grinning at me as he brought me into his side. He tugged at my hair. "Took you long enough, dove. I was about to send a search party in there after you."

Because he'd been waiting *so* long. I mean class just got out, but the retort shut down in my throat the moment he folded his hand behind my neck. He pulled me into a kiss that set my body ablaze, his big arms caging me into his harsh heat. His teeth tugged my bottom lip as he pulled away, and after, he took my things and escorted me outside. I told him about Professor Hershel mentioning my term paper as we walked, and he basically took all the credit in so many arrogant words. I shoved his chest. "I did write it you know."

"But without me..." He touched his chest, jostling me before dashing his eyebrows up. "Anyway, you done for the day? Was going to take you out for dinner or something."

"Is that an *actual* invite for a date or..."

"Don't with the mouth." He held mine, grinning as he tugged my lip down. "And yeah, it's a date. You got plans?"

Since I did, I nodded. "I do actually. *Real* busy."

"Doing what?" He actually appeared shocked, his eyebrows hard when they narrowed in.

I rolled my eyes. "Just busy."

"Really? Well, cancel them because you're now busy with me." His arms fell around my body, and I was definitely tempted, definitely *hot* when my body turned into ooze as he braced his mighty palms on my ass. I'd been letting him play a lot with that lately.

What could I say, I really liked it.

I wasn't sure I could turn him down again as sexy as he was and the fact his hands were all over me, but it was made a little easier to pull away when a car pulled up in front of us on the street. The old station wagon I definitely recognized, my mom behind it and my stepdad Ben in the passenger seat.

"Knight Reed as I live and breath," Mom stated, her eyes dancing with delight. She really was happy to see him, her hands flailing after she parked, and I rolled my eyes.

Lowering to the level of the car, Knight smiled at her. "Hey, Ms. Michaelson. Good to see you."

"Good to see you and it's Ms. Michaelson-*Harris* now." She grinned. "Greer told us you were going to school here too."

"Hey, Greer!" Ben bopped forward in the front seat, waving at me like a loon in his cop uniform, and could I be more embarrassed in the middle of the street with Knight Reed beside me?

I waved a little. "Hey, Ben." I pointed to Knight. "This is Knight. Knight Reed, my stepdad Ben."

Ben tipped his chin. "Sup, man."

And as corny as that sounded, Knight managed to keep his shit together, his smile widening as he lifted a hand to Ben. "Nice to meet you. Greer told me about you."

"Did she?" Mom asked, and all too quickly, she noticed Knight's hand, a hand that very much cuffed my arm. He hadn't let go after I pulled away, and needless to say, the 'rents noticed. I could have palmed my face as both Mom and Ben grinned like fiends. Mom flashed hers over to Knight. "How about you join us for dinner, Knight? Would love to catch up. Hear about how you're doing? We're expecting Greer this evening, and you should come too."

I chewed my lip when Knight looked at me. I shrugged. "Told you I was busy."

"Well, I'm still not." And dropping an arm around my shoulders, Knight grinned at my mom. "I'd love to. I mean, as long as Greer doesn't mind."

"Of course she doesn't. Both of you get in. We'll take you back to the home front."

Dear God. Lifting my eyes to the heavens, I watched Knight chuckle as he escorted me over to my mom's car. "Sorry in advance," I told him, to which he shrugged.

He tugged my chin. "You're overreacting. I remember your mom being cool."

Maybe but watching Knight Reed force his huge, line-backer-sized body into my mom's beat-up station wagon was the stuff of sheer modification. Tucked in at my side, he dropped his arm around me again, and I got to hear all Mom and Ben's questions about that on the way to their house. Yeah, tonight was definitely about to be fun.

CHAPTER
NINETEEN

Greer

Mom and Ben basically talked Knight's ear off over spaghetti and meatballs, and Knight seemed to not only entertain the probing about how he was doing and what he was into now, but appeared to get sheer delight out of it. I think mostly because he saw it bugged me, that mischief obviously still there, but since them interrogating him about his day to day laid them off me for a night I went gratefully along with it. The pair shockingly didn't poke Knight and me about what we were too much, and I was grateful for that because I had no idea *what* we were. He'd only just asked me out on an actual date tonight, so pardon either of us if we weren't trying to walk down the aisle quite yet.

Currently, Ben filled Knight's ear about campus police stuff, thanking him profusely for the squad's new gear like Knight had actually had a hand in any of that. My stepdad was basically brown-nosing to hell, and if I could shut off my eardrums, I would, shaking my head with a smile over dishes. Mom and I had taken them after we'd all finished up, and I was currently helping her load the dishwasher.

Mom passed a glance over to Knight and Ben from the kitchen into the living room. She smiled. "Well, he seems happy. Knight?"

Did he?

I swung my gaze around, Knight's elbow propped on the table as he continued to watch my stepdad fall all over himself in front of him. Noticing me, Knight winked in my direction before going back to the conversation, and Mom grinned, noticing that too.

"That because of you?" she asked, and I rolled my eyes.

"I don't know, Mom. I guess he seems happy." He seemed something, all right. Not nearly as moody. I smiled to myself as Mom handed me a dish to load.

"I hope you're being safe."

"Mom!"

"What, honey bug?" She nudged me. "I'm just saying, guys did not look like that when I went to community college for the time I did."

"Oh, that's nice. I'm sure Ben would love that."

She play shoved me. "Now, I'm not talking about Ben and you know that. I'm just saying. If you're having sex, just make sure you're taking care of all that."

I so was not having this conversation with her right now, my face way too heated and though she obviously noticed that too at least she ignored that fact. She rinsed another dish before handing it to me, shrugging. "It's just nice that it seems like he's okay is all. He's been dealt a rough hand in life, that boy."

"You mean his parents?" I asked. "His mom?"

"You know about that?"

I nodded. "He actually took me to see her recently. Thought it might help me with my paper for psych class."

This seemed to surprise her completely, as she turned

around and rested her hip against the counter. "You mean, she's still around? It's just been so long. I figured…"

Probably what most would, that eventually they might take her off her life support. I wet my lips. "He said it's been twelve years."

Mom frowned, tsking before shaking her head. "I always hoped for the best for him. That can't have been easy, and right after his dad passed. Poor thing."

I hadn't heard much about his dad besides the fact he'd had a riding accident. She'd obviously kept that and details of his mom away from me, and I guessed I wasn't surprised because of the tender age I was when I knew him. I just always figured his grandpa raised him, didn't think about much else really.

Our dishes clanked as we kept loading dishes. I took one from Mom. "And you're not mad about what happened? I mean, he basically got you fired."

She tsked again before rolling her eyes. "Bug, he was child. And… sometimes things are just complicated."

"How so?"

She placed a hand on the counter. "Just complicated. And as far as I'm concerned, a boy loses his family that young and acts out I don't blame him. I don't blame him for a lot of things, and I'm definitely not mad."

She nearly scolded me, and I felt bad, staring away.

Mom squeezed my shoulder. "Anyway, I think we need to go save him from Ben," she said, nudging me with a smile. "Finish up in here, and I'll serve the pie."

She took it off the counter, store-bought but so good none of that mattered. My mom always made do for us, was completely awesome and more so than I believed. She really held no ill will, sympathetic where I might not have been if I'd been in her situation.

But I guess now I knew all the facts too.

After I started the dishwasher, I wiped my hands,

deciding to check my phone before heading back out. I got an email so I checked it, really surprised to hear from Professor Hershel at all, least of all so soon. I'd just sent him an email with all my research notes earlier that day from my phone since I had the file saved to the Cloud.

Professor Hershel: Good work on this paper, Ms. Michaelson. I just finished it and loved it. I can't post grades until I finish everyone else's, but yes, it was outstanding.

A little happy dance I jigged on the inside, reading on.

Professor Hershel: And I went over your notes. Excellent stuff too, which makes sense why the paper was so good. You might want to consider a degree in psychology or even further, going the route of a medical doctor. You've obviously taken to all this.

Never thought I'd hear that. I smiled on, but the expression left a little by how he left the email.

Professor Hershel: Also, I think I might have heard you wrong before when we were talking. You said your friend's mom was in a coma due to a head injury, but from what I can see with what you gave me, her coma is medically induced.

What?

Professor Hershel: Though maybe I don't have all the facts or you jotted something down wrong error-wise in your notes. Either way, excellent work, and I'll see you back in class next week.

Knight

I slow-fucked Greer, being inside this girl ridiculous. I'd merely get a taste, then have to be right back in, barely getting inside her dorm tonight before we were in her bed. Gripping her hands with one of my fists, I extended her, that petite little body shaking beneath me. Dipping my head, I laved over her pebbled breasts, tugging one of her pert nipples into my mouth. "Relax, dove. Last I checked, I'd popped that cherry already."

Despite that, she was always still a quivering mess with me, innocence laced in something backed by fire. That hellcat kicked me with her little toes after I called her out, but I pulled that sigh right back out of her mouth when I bit one of those feisty little lips of hers.

"Shut up and just fuck me," she commanded, wriggling beneath my weight. Putting up with that mouth this time, I grabbed her, pulling her back with me when I settled on my hunches.

I slammed into her body, bouncing her up and down as my dick disappeared in and out of her. This wouldn't be long. I didn't have the stamina. This girl may be tiny, but I worked myself like a fucking machine just to come as hard as I could when I was with her. I didn't want to waste it, all of it too sweet.

"Fuck, Knight. Fuck." Her nails tore across my back, and I roared, Greer dipping that sea of blond to bite my shoulder. She broke skin easily and not only did that make me want to fuck her harder but lose my mind myself. Palming her ass, I slapped myself against her inner thighs, the skin red and harsh from repeated impact. I could only take so much of this before I needed that ass, sticking my fingers inside.

She called out into my mouth, her lip pulled between my teeth. I grinned. "Hope you're ready, dove."

Because I was coming *hard* and with so much force, I feared I might shoot through the damn condom. I needed to get this girl on birth control, a fail condom inevitable with as hard and frequently as I fucked her. My little Greer definitely wasn't a virgin anymore, all mine, and I needed her like I needed something akin to life. Food didn't even taste the same to me anymore. Not since I had her. It was harshly different, fucking scary, but so greedy, I went along for the ride.

I think it was safe to say I wasn't the only one.

She fell back as she came herself, her body stretched and bowed in my arms. I slapped once, twice, milking her for all I could take. My eyes rolling back, I was shaky myself as I watched her come apart then later back to me. I grinned as I pulled her up, tasting her lips and started to roll back in the bed with her before she eased from underneath me.

Before I knew it, she was starting to put her clothes on, dress herself like she was some quick fuck for me. She'd never been that with me, no matter how much I'd led her to believe that when it came to similar things in the past. I was well aware I'd messed a few things up before, and looking back, I was definitely not proud of that. I reacted with fear a lot when it came to her. My default sometimes and Royal was right. When it came to women, sometimes I was just scared to hold on too tight to them. Anything could be taken away, a harsh reality I knew.

"Everything all right?" I touched her back, her clothes back on, and I didn't like that. I pinched at her top. "You've been different since we got back from your mom and Ben's."

She barely spoke to me in the car ride back here, normally so talkative I couldn't get her to slow down. It balanced well with me since when it came to conversation, I'd rather listen than be a part. Anyway, after we got back here, I'd started to talk to her, but once we'd realized her dorm was empty, I had a one-track mind. I'd poked at her for her body, and then, well, no conversation. I hadn't thought it weird at first.

But now, she was getting up. She turned. "Want a drink? I want a drink."

She didn't wait for my response before leaving the room, and lifting my eyes, something did feel wrong. I got up myself, quickly tossing away the condom before putting my clothes back on and following after her. I found her back out in her dorm's common area, head dipped inside the fridge. I lounged against a wall in the kitchen. "I feel like something's going on. You mad at me? Mad I took up your mom's invite for dinner?"

Yeah, I had taken it because it'd seemed she hadn't wanted me there. But then again, that was our dynamic. I poked, bugging her, and she ran her mouth, bugging the shit out of me. We didn't work unless we were arguing or handling each other. Greer stayed in the fridge, her sigh hard. "I just want a drink."

"Okay." Pushing off the wall, I helped her, taking the bottle of juice from her when she rose with it. I served her, then served myself, the pair of us taking it back into the common area.

Plopping on her couch, I took her with me, putting my juice on the coffee table and reaching for my controller. I queued up a game since I kept the system over here, playing around Greer's body for a while. She drank her juice, leaning back into me, and eventually, she was looking up at me. She looked so sad it actually pissed me off. Why was she sad?

What the fuck did I do?

It was crazy I even cared, so different now, but seeing her sad truly did piss me off. I didn't think I had done anything, *which meant* something outside of me did something to her. *That's* what pissed me off. That I might have to do something about it and hurt someone.

"What's going on?" I asked again, and though I let the game play, my attention was on nothing but her. Her when she put her cup down and eased her arms around me, her when her body shook again and I wasn't even fucking her. Worried now, I put the controller down. "Greer? What the fuck? You're kind of scaring me."

"I am scared," she said, and at that moment, I realized she was crying. *Fucking crying*, with tears in her eyes. The sheen made them starkly blue, and she squeezed them. "Knight…"

What. The. Hell? Everything had been fine before we came here tonight and I rose up, taking her with me.

She shook her head. "I... I just need to talk to you about something."

Dread, like harsh to my core. Girls didn't say that shit unless something was up. I just never cared about that before, girls easy. A dime a dozen, but it was never easy with Greer. It was fucking harder, and I worked so hard not to be who I usually was with her. In fact, it pulled at me so much every day. I wanted to be abrasive, a jerk. It was just my MO because feeling things, feeling *this* was the harsh opposite of the good feeling. You couldn't get one without the other in a relationship, hence why I always stayed the fuck away from them.

I folded a hand behind her back. "Talk."

Instead, she reached over and grabbed her phone, showing it to me. "I got an email from my psych professor."

That's what this was? I smiled a little. "You get a bad grade or something?" I knew she took all this shit way more seriously than me, but what the hell? "They'll be other ways to pad your grade. If you want I can even talk to…"

Then I read the conversation, an email he'd sent her. It talked about what a good job she'd done on her term paper. Shit, yeah she had. I helped her.

But then I read on, scanning as it came to the part about things that had nothing to do with her, things that had to do with my family and me. I lifted my gaze, my eyes narrow. "You told him about my mom?"

"I took lots of notes at the nursing home." Panicked, she waved her arms. Her face had shifted into at least three variations of cherry red, her palms going to her teary eyes. "He thought it was fascinating because he used to work with coma patients. After I turned in my paper, he wanted to know more."

All right. No big. I shook my head. "Why the tears?"

"Did you see what the email said?" She put it in front of my face again. "The part about the coma? He thinks it's medically induced, and I don't know what that means, Knight. But that's weird, right? You said the coma was from trauma… not that."

But I also saw she could have been mistaken, copied her notes down wrong like he said. Maybe she thought she heard something different when speaking to my mom's doctors. I framed her face. "I'm sure you just misheard. How many doctors and medical staff did you interview that day? I'm sure you just wrote down something wrong like your professor mentioned."

But then she tapped around on her phone again, showing me something she definitely shouldn't have. She had a picture of a chart in her phone, *my mom's* name in the top corner.

My mouth parted. "Why do you have this?"

Her knees came up, and she cradled them. "I… I thought it would be help—"

"You're not listening to me." She moved off my lap, to my side and I basically put her there. I put the phone in her face. "Why do you have a picture of one of my mom's fucking medical charts? You shouldn't even have access to that. What the fuck, Greer?"

"I just stumbled upon it. I swear. It was just sitting there in a pocket next to your mom's bed. Maybe one of the nurses or doctors left it there or something—"

"And so that meant you should take fucking pictures of it!" Enraged, *livid* as my body heat traveled a million and a half fucking degrees. "What right did you fucking have?"

"I didn't. Fuck." She covered her face, opening her hands. "It was out of line, but that doesn't deny what I read. What I saw right there." She pointed to the picture. "I didn't copy anything down wrong, Knight. It's all right there, facts."

"And it's still probably a fucking error." I didn't want to

look at what she was showing me anymore, the lies and invasiveness...

The betrayal.

She showed her professor this, my family just a pack of freaks for her viewing pleasure. Her term paper had been about general psychology terms, not prying into my goddamn life. I got up, finished with this shit.

"Knight, *please.* Just listen to me!"

Hence, the reason for her tears. She obviously didn't want to show me this, worried how I'd react, and she should have been worried.

She should fear.

I grabbed my coat, ignoring her as I left the dorm room and slammed the door. I hoped she got a good grade on her term paper.

I hoped it was all fucking worth it.

CHAPTER
TWENTY

Knight

My grandpa called the next day, asking me if I wanted to go to New York City with him for the day. He was going into town for business, and since I needed something to do besides dwell on bullshit, I took him up on the offer, readily taking the car he sent for me. I met him up at the airport, and we had a nice calm ride through the air on private charter, barely talking and just hanging out. That's how things used to be way back when before school and women got in the way. It was just Gramps and me, simpler.

I wished for simpler times again as I let him go about his day. I didn't attend his business meetings with him, of course, opting out to shop and hang out in the city. But once all that concluded for him, we ended up at the flower market. Gramps didn't do much of his own gardening, but he liked to pick out blooms personally when he wanted them. I stayed nearby as he thumbed petals for the flower boxes at the house, giving my opinion when asked. I wasn't really into all that shit, but did enjoy just being near him, near family. Some things were obviously put into perspective recently.

My fingers thumbed my phone screen, distracted a little when he asked me my opinion this time. I pointed at one bunch in his hand. "Red looks good."

My grandpa merely chuckled in response, *knowing* I didn't know anything about this shit. Even still, he asked and I appreciated that. His house was my house too, always would be. He pinched a bud. "I'll make a note, son. I'm thinking we need more in the gardens too."

I headed over to look at what he wanted for that, more reds, pinks, and even some teals. He had his assistant Joshua with him so anytime he liked something or stopped to look, Joshua made a note. I supposed I'd have a Joshua one day, why I was getting my business degree to take over things one day. My family's presence was very prominent in my small town. We owned many business just like the Prinzes, my boy Royal's family.

When I missed another cue for my opinion about the flowers, my grandpa turned, smiling at me. "You've been distracted, yes?"

I had, but also had too much pride to agree. I shrugged. "Nothing to be concerned about."

"Is it school?" He waved a hand for Joshua to do what he wished, and the guy nodded like the manservant he was, leaving us before ducking behind a set of bushes out of sight. Having people around to serve me and my family was just something that came along with the territory of my life, used to it since I always had been around it. Grandfather frowned. "You haven't mentioned anything."

That was because I hadn't been talking to him, lying to him a lot lately by keeping things from him. With this whole thing with Greer, I'd basically become obsessed over keeping what she'd seen that night at the frat quiet, but eventually, it turned into something completely else. More obsession.

Then later bullshit.

She'd put me completely on fire, and I could only be mad at myself. I'd shared that part of myself with her, gave her details about my family when it'd been none of her goddamn business, and she'd not only used it against me but betrayed me. She'd actually had the nerve to text and call me after I'd left her dorm yesterday. She'd said she was sorry for prying, just wanted to talk to me like she had a fucking right. She'd betrayed my trust, point blank. My jaw moved. "School's not bothering me."

"So what is?"

I shook my head, and once again, he smiled. His hands rested on his cane. "You know you are so much like your father. So strong-willed."

Chuckling, I scratched the side of my neck with a finger. "You say that all the time."

"Because it's true." He tapped his cane in my direction before using it to bring his arm around me. "Couldn't take care of him. No one could because…"

"He was too busy being stubborn," I said, having heard this all before. "And taking care of everyone else."

"A fierce protector, that one." His eyes warmed. "He'd run into the fire for someone he cared about, getting so deep before he realized doing so could swallow him whole. By then, of course, it's always too late, isn't it?"

"Yes." I'd heard this story too, many, many times. Dad had reacted. He hadn't waited around, and Gramps said when Dad had been a kid, that shit had gotten him in trouble— often. I could definitely relate. My hands slid into his pockets. "But how do you keep from getting burnt?"

"You don't, and that makes for a hell of a life, doesn't it?"

A hell of a short life in my dad's case, gone way too soon. His accident had nothing to do with him being rash, but he had been adventurous. Always wanting to take chances, and that was something even I remembered about him.

Grandpa shook me and, after directing Joshua back, asked if I wanted to get dinner before leaving the city. I was always fucking famished so of course, I said sure. We had a favorite burger place we both liked to go when we were in town, and after Joshua had our car come around and filled with flowers, we headed over to it from the market, the sedan fragrant with my grandpa's blooms.

"Have you thought any more about your mom?" Gramps asked me inside. I'd been on my phone again and looked up. He frowned. "I don't want to pressure you but..."

The decision did need to be made, and I needed to stop being such a goddamn priss and make it. Maybe if I did let Mom go, we *both* could move on. Grandfather and I would be able to grieve, and Mom, well, she could be with Dad in our family plot. Letting her go was the responsible thing to do.

My hand gripped my phone. "Probably should."

"Yeah?" Leaning in, Grandfather squeezed my shoulder. "I just don't want the decision plaguing you. I feel like it has a potential to be that."

He was right, of course, and even in this short time of consideration, that's exactly what it'd been doing. I think I knew that's where things were heading all along, and there'd definitely been a reason I hadn't been able to go and see her lately. It just hurt seeing her that way. It hurt every damn time. I nodded again. "I think it's best. And you're right it's... it's time."

"You're sure?"

"I'm sure."

Grandfather didn't say anything else as he let go of my shoulder, but I knew he'd take care of all the arrangements. He was like my dad and me, that protector part we obviously got from somewhere. Where I failed in the end was I decided to protect the wrong person, and as we headed toward the restaurant, I decided to ask my grandpa a question. He was always asking about what kinds of programs and departments I felt needed attention on campus, funding. Since I was there, he felt I had insights where he didn't, and in the past, I'd been reluctant to share my thoughts. Even more so about the departments money should be taken away from, scaled back…

"Grandfather, I think some money should be moved around. Money you give to the school?" I said, and once his brow lifted, I continued. "Obviously, this is just all my opinion. But I'm wondering if Pembroke needs as much as they do in some departments…"

CHAPTER
TWENTY-ONE

Greer

I spotted Knight on a transition between classes. I was cutting across the quad, and he was walking along the concrete path, his grandpa Gerald beside him. They were amongst a group, a bunch of other old guys also wearing suits and walking about this place like they owned it.

I guessed in a way they did.

I was hot fire as I bee-lined in that direction, unavailable to think straight. Hell, even see straight because if I had, I might have considered my next move. If I had, I wouldn't have waltzed right up to Knight Reed…

And slapped him across his gorgeous face.

He hadn't seen it coming at all, of course, gripping his jaw, and my hand burning at my side, and I literally thought about what I'd done after. I thought about what would come next and what that would mean. This guy had done a lot of damage already.

Well, I could do more.

Scorching rage in his eyes as he turned back, and many of

the older men with him gasped. One of which had been his grandfather, completely stunned with that cane in his hands. His salt and pepper eyes narrowed. "Young lady, what is the meaning of this!"

My fist clenched, ready to strike again, but Knight got my arm before I could lift it. He pulled me, jerked me so hard I thought my arm might pull right out of its socket. He had me by the shoulders as he pushed me away from the old guys, the older men talking amongst themselves while Knight skirted me away from the crowd. He basically tossed me behind a tree, and when I came for him again, not only did he get my wrist, he pulled me up to meet his face.

His expression could have frightened even the most wicked man.

"I let you have that one, dove," he announced, throwing my arm away from him. He darted a finger. "But hit me the fuck again, and I don't know what that will mean for you."

He was literally the worst, literally the most fucked-up human being on the planet. How else could he explain what he did to me, did to Mom, Ben, and me. My eyes watered. "How dare you? How fucking dare you—"

"Young lady, I'll ask you to calm down, or I will have to call campus security for you."

Gerald Reed strolling across the quad, clearly the representative amongst the old guys. The rest of them congregated out of the fray while Mr. Reed strode off to obviously see what was up, but on the ball, Knight didn't let him get within many feet of me before jerking me away. He raised a hand. "I'm handling this, Grandfather. You don't need to worry."

"And what's to be handled?" The older man came forward, raising his chin. "What is this, son—"

"*This*," I said, working Knight's hands off me, "is your grandson being a complete and utter dick."

"I recognize you, don't I?" Mr. Reed asked, then lift his

chin again. "You were at the frat house the other night when I'd been there."

"She was, but she doesn't mean anything." Again, with the disrespect. Again with him being a complete jerk to me when it hadn't been warranted at all. I *never* asked to stand between him and Bryce, to come across what I'd seen that horrible night.

My lips quivered. "How could you, Knight?"

He faced me then, looked me clear in my eyes. His hand lowered from his grandpa's direction. "I'm assuming this is about *my family's* decision to redirect some of *its* funds."

"Redirection?" Mr. Reed exchanged a glance between us, then sighed as his attention drifted to me. "If the reallocation of the monies has affected you negatively, I'm sorry. The Reed family puts its money where it feels its needed more when it comes to campus activities and programs. I'm sure you understand."

I didn't because that decision didn't just adversely affect me, it shattered me. Both me and *my* family. "That money you scaled back siphoned directly from the campus police department and maintenance staff. *That money* paid for my mom and stepdad to have jobs. They've now been let go. *Done,* and since they don't have jobs, I can't go to school here next term!"

Mom and Ben basically told me last night, called me over for dinner and everything when it hadn't even been our night to eat together. They'd urged it, telling me they needed to see me and it was important.

"I'm so sorry, honey bug," Mom had said, looking truly sick. She'd sighed. *"These things just happen sometimes, but we'll bounce back, and if you can't return to Pembroke next semester, we'll see what we can do for next year. I'm just... I'm just so sorry."*

No, these things didn't just happen. They didn't just occur out of the ether and completely due to chance and circumstance. I had higher odds getting hit by lightning and setting myself on fire.

Maybe in a way I had.

I did the minute I got involved with Knight Reed, an arrogant fuck who not only looked at me right now with zero remorse, but was completely blinded. This had nothing to do with my parents, only me, and this may have been his family's money, but the decision was definitely influenced by him, had to be.

Knight said nothing in response to what I said and his grandpa between us, it was him to actually step forward. Mr. Reed frowned. "I understand your anger, but if the school felt the need for cutbacks, that has nothing to do with the Reed family. Least of all my grandson."

"All do respect, sir? I think it does." My lip quivered as my gaze shift to Knight. My eyes narrowed. "How could you? How *fucking* could you! We get in an argument, and you do this?"

"You're embarrassing yourself." Knight's eyes darkened in my direction, his face red and flushed from where I'd struck him. His jaw worked. "Now, I suggest you take you and your little tirade somewhere else before it gets you in trouble. You have no right speaking to me or my grandpa this way."

I hadn't disrespected his grandpa, the only one really disrespected in this situation was me. I came to him with something, and not only had he disregarded it, but punished me for it.

Knight's hand touched his grandpa's arm, the two of them starting to walk away.

"Your dad would be real proud, you know?" I stated. "About who you turned out to be?"

Eyes wild, Knight shot them in my direction. His grandpa frowned again. "What is she talking about, son?"

"Nothing, Grandfather. I'll take care of this."

Knight strode away from him quickly, back to me and this time, he kept things between us, snatching me up and making me stay behind the tree. He put a finger in my face. "You know *nothing* about my family."

"I know enough." I wet my lips. "And maybe those monsters in the dark from your hometown... maybe you fit right in with them."

His hand curled at his side, that King ring he'd talked about shining over his finger. Yeah, he fit right in with them. Yeah, those were definitely his people.

Knight pushed off the tree without another word from me, clearly simmering in heat as he stalked away. He'd found his place, and it clearly wasn't with me.

I think in the end I'd been the one to gratefully benefit.

CHAPTER
TWENTY-TWO

Knight

"And this year's humanitarian award goes to Gerald Reed!!"

The room erupted in applause when Grandfather's name was called, and I stood, right next to him. He eased out of his chair, holding back his tie, but before going up on stage he shook my hand, giving me a hug. He always acknowledged me first, always.

I led the room in applause after he broke away from me, always the loudest in the room whenever my Grandfather was acknowledged for anything he did, whether it was business related or otherwise. In this case, he'd been one of the lead backers for the research and development department at Pembroke University's medical school, and needless to say, the grant committee had been pleased. They held this luncheon every year, but this had been the first year Grandfather had been recognized for his role in everything. That's not why he did the things he did to help, of course, but it was nice to *see* him be acknowledged. He worked hard and took care of many people.

He got up on stage, in a dark suit like mine, and after the room quieted a little, I eased back in my chair, the rest of the room doing the same. Grandfather was handed a crystal award in the shape of a bird, a dove, and I felt some irony in that for myself. I thought about Greer more than I liked these days, what she was doing.

Putting her out of my mind now and respecting this moment for my grandpa, I sat back while Grandfather took pictures with the award for the cameras. After, he approached the podium with it, a smile on his face.

"I'd liked to dedicate this award to my grandson," he said, putting the award out toward me. He could see me easily, smiling at me in the afternoon lit room. "He inspires me every day, such strength for such a young man."

I clapped before everyone else once again, the room following behind me. Grandfather entertained several pictures at the podium before returning back to our table. The room had a nice lunch, and though I never usually went to stuffy events like this, I enjoyed hearing about the things the medical school did. A lot of the money that went there funded research for coma patients, a big reason why I'd decided to go to school here, outside of the obvious legacy thing. I believed, maybe one day, I'd have a chance to have my mom come back to me. That *maybe* I could do something for her one day.

Swallowing, I smiled as Grandfather pulled me into a picture with his award. Some of the alumni wanted it, the pictures snapped quickly after the luncheon concluded. Of course, they wanted even more with my grandpa, but I got a text from Royal and got distracted, letting Grandfather do his thing as I looked at my phone.

My chest squeezed.

Royal: Hey. You around? I got that stuff you were looking for.

I had my buddy look into my mom's medical records. He'd said he had a guy who might be able to help with that.

Royal always had "a guy" and I'd be lying if I said his resources hadn't been useful in the past. He and the rest of our close friends had a pretty dark history when it came to our hometown and the Court affiliation we came from.

I thumbed my phone.

Me: What did you find?

Royal: Can I call you?

Chest squeezed again, but as it seemed grandpa was dealing with his many admirers, I excused myself.

"Everything okay?" he asked me after, so concerned despite being surrounded by his adoring fans.

I waved him off, my phone to my ear. "Yeah, just Royal. Texted me something so I was gonna call him. I'll make it quick."

With Grandfather's blessing, I took the call outside the ballroom, hand shoved in my pocket. My heart was beating a mile a minute, worried that Royal actually found something and I might have to lose my shit. I'd asked him to look into my mom's medical stuff for merely peace of mind. Grandfather and I were about to take her off life support soon, and I just needed to know.

And Greer Michaelson got inside my head again.

But could she be right? I hoped not as much as I did. If there was some foul play here, that meant the doctors handling my mom's case couldn't be trusted. That meant something was going on here...

I shook my head, ahead of myself when I should be talking to my friend. "What do you got? Did you find something?"

"Not sure yet."

"What do you mean not sure?"

"I mean, I got the email with the e-file and didn't open it. All this shit is obviously private." He blew a breath into the phone. "I felt you should be the one to open it. Whatever you find."

And here I thought he actually found something. God, fuck.

I slammed a hand against one of the building's walls, calming the hell down.

"Jesus, kid. I thought you'd found something," I said, releasing a breath. "You scared the shit out of me."

"Well, I might have reason, but like I said, this is all you. You should be the one to look at everything."

He wanted to respect me, my privacy, and suddenly, I felt like a fool again. I had him look into all this, all this shit obviously paranoia. I scrubbed my hand through my hair. "You know, what? Forget about it?"

"Forget about it?"

I nodded even though he couldn't see. "It was me being paranoid. Like I said, Greer was saying shit, and it got to me."

I'd told him everything, of course, since he'd asked why I needed what I'd asked. He'd looked into it right away after that, but I knew he would have regardless. Royal Prinze was ride or die, our other close friends LJ and Jax the same. We'd do anything for each other, completely brothers without the blood.

"But what if she had something there?" he asked. "What if she's right?"

That meant more than just her being right. It meant foul play, and how could anything be foul under my grandpa's watch? He'd hired the best doctors. He'd *cared* for my mom after all these years and put her in that fancy nursing home with the best doctors money could buy. He had some flown out from other countries just to care for her. A strike against the doctors who helped my mom was one against my grandpa, and that just wasn't something I could accept. There was no way something like that could get past him.

There was just no way.

I moved my jaw, no words, and Royal breathed through the phone.

"You know what?" he asked. "I'll just hold onto everything. No rush, you know?"

He knew exactly what he needed to do without asking, my fingers gripping into my hair. "Thanks, man. I appreciate it."

"Of course. Love you, guy."

How funny, as he'd never say that shit before December came into his life. He'd opened up a lot. "Same, bro. Take care."

"Take care."

In the car, Grandfather went over the events while I'd been away, talked about the discussions he'd had and even the celebrities who'd approached him at the event. Everyone wanted a piece of him, trying to get close to that power, and I was in awe of him every day. He influenced many people, moved a lot of mountains, and that was definitely a lot to live up to. His window eased down as he lit a cigar, a celebratory one he'd said he received from the governor. "The governor's invited us for dinner this weekend at his home with his wife. I was thinking as long as you're not too busy with your studies?"

Always accommodating me first, I smiled, telling him that was fine, and my phone buzzed as he took a call. Another one of his adoring fans no doubt, and as he took that, I gazed at my device.

Royal: Sorry, buddy. I took a look at the email. Couldn't help it. Thought you wouldn't mind? Felt like you might have needed that.

Actually feeling I kind of did, I sat up. I started to text him back, but his text message bubble returned.

Royal: Anyway, I'm glad did. I'm sending you this file over—ASAP and buddy, you seriously need to look at it and get your legal team involved. Your mom's coma is medically induced. She came out of her actual coma only eight days after her accident. It says so in the file.

What the fuck?

Royal: Doctors put her right back under. No explanation.

But there had to be one, right? I mean, there had to be a reason a doctor would put a patient back under after a traumatic event...

Right?

A slow panic enveloped me, another text from Royal coming in.

Royal: Anyway, call me after you look at it. This is seriously fucked. Someone might be purposely hurting your mom, bro.

My hand gripped my phone, about to shatter the thing into fucking pieces, and it took me a second to realize my grandpa called my name, and by then, I was shaking.

Gramps wet his lips, his cell phone in his hand. He covered the receiver upon seeing me. "Chicken or beef, son?"

"What?"

He frowned. "The governor's wife... she wants to know chicken or beef for Saturday night?"

My lips closed, fucking frazzled. I started to say something before my grandpa went ahead and put the phone back to his ear.

"We'll call you back with the decision," he said, thanking whoever for their time before hanging up. He leaned over. "What's happening? You look completely shaken, Knight."

Did I? Needing to pound something, I took the frustrations out on my phone, the device digging so hard in my hand I thought I'd actually break it.

"Knight?"

I panned, facing him. "I just got a text from Royal. I asked him to get a copy of Mom's medical records. I wanted to see them."

"And why's that?" His body shifted in my direction, his cane under his palms. "Why would you do that? Why the need for that?"

The reaction floored me, the quickness of it, and he immediately saw that all over my face, his eyes twitching wide before he panned away. The pair of us bumped in the car, running over uneven ground, and I couldn't see anymore, not anything at all.

"Grandfather?" The word was a whisper in my voice, *strained* to fucking hell. I pulled my fingers through my hair, restless and at a loss for words. I forced some. "Do you know what he found out?"

Absolutely nothing on his end, *fucking nothing*, and I didn't understand.

I decided to try again.

"I said do you know what he found out—"

"Of course I know."

Shock ripped through me, immediately but not just by his candor. The lack of emotion, the lack of anything at all got me. This information should floor him as much as it did me. Piss him off. This was his son's wife.

This was my mom.

He *loved her*, didn't he? I didn't see that as his hand lifted, rubbing his face with a sigh. His hand fell. "Son, before you say anything else. You don't know all the facts."

All the facts? All the damn facts were that my mom was in a coma when she didn't need to be. A coma *he* told me to pull the plug on not days ago. My mouth moved. "What facts, Grandfather? Mom's in a coma when she doesn't have to be…"

"And that's the hand she was dealt."

"Hand? What hand? How? Grandfather, I don't understand—"

"She tried to take you away from me!"

His voice raised when never in my whole life had I ever heard it. Even when disciplining me growing up, I'd never heard it. A sternness, yes, but never an octave above calm and cool. That was just my grandpa, Gerald Reed, nothing if not calm.

His hand warmed the top of his cane, the opposite now. I shook my head. "What are you talking about?"

"Just as I said." He nodded as he faced me. "Your mom tried to take you away. Ran off with you into the night. Did you know you were in the car with her that night? She could have killed you both."

I did know, but from what I remembered, my injuries had been minor. Honestly a lot of that was fuzzy, so long ago.

"She ran off with you," he continued on. "She didn't want you growing up privileged. Wanted you to be trash like her."

"What are you talking about—"

"You mom was a whore," he gritted, my eyes twitched wide. His jaw worked. "Your father's whore. He hired an escort for an event, then had the nerve to fall in love with her."

I hadn't known that, none of it. They'd all gotten along, though. My parents and my grandpa, no arguments ever in my house between anyone growing up. My mouth parted. "You acted like you cared about her."

"I cared for you." His expression hardened, cold. "I cared for my son, and though I didn't agree with his choice, I allowed it. I let him marry his whore."

My nostrils flared. "Don't call her that."

"That's what she was son, *is*. She's *Pretty Woman* in real frickin' life. She was trash and I let it go, but I didn't have to after your father died. I didn't have to pretend it was okay. She had no means *at all* to take care of you outside of what she was left from your father, and hell if I was going to let her squander his trust away."

"So you did this to her—"

"She did this to herself." He threw a hand out. "She wanted to leave with you. Take you to God only knew where to come out any which way. Thought she could because she had your father's money and believed she could do it. She couldn't take care of herself before she married your father, so pardon me if I had no confidence in her abilities. I got the courts involved. Wanted custody of you and a say in how you grew up. *That's* when she ran. That's when she got in that car accident with you and ended up in that coma."

"But she didn't stay that way," I charged. "She woke up. Royal said she woke up!"

"And would have taken you again, rest assured." No emotion, none at all. He shook his head. "*That* wasn't going to happen. Not on my watch. I did what I had to do. I did what I needed to do…"

To protect me, and so a Reed once again ends up in the flames of hell. Surging, I turned my head, all I could do to keep from doing something else.

"Twelve years," I whispered, fucking shaking. "Twelve years and what? I turn off her life support, and she wakes up?"

"I would have taken care of that."

I panned, seeing the first of anything at all in his eyes. It was fear, actual terror and staring straight at me. His jaw moved. "After you gave me the okay, I would have taken care of the rest."

Meaning he would have ended her himself, finished the job with no chance at all for my mom to come out of her darkness. Who knew if she even could at this point? She'd been under so damn long, and that had to have done something.

"You were going to let me kill her," I said, mortified as I stared at him. "You were going to let me kill my own mother."

"No, son. No." He put a hand on my shoulder, squeezing. "I told you. I would have—"

"But you left the decision up to me!" I forced his hand off me. I put mine to my chest. "*I* would have made the call. I would have killed my own mom and thought I was saving her by taking her out of that fucking darkness she's been in for over half my life."

More emotion, more fear in his eyes. His swallow was hard. "Knight—"

"I can't believe Greer was right."

"Greer? Greer who? Greer Michaelson? That little girl whose mother used to work for us? What does she have to do with anything—"

"Stop the car!" I cut him off when I rose my hand, the car still moving. "Stop the fucking car or I'm getting out in the middle of traffic."

"Stop the car, Nigel. Damn you." It screeched to a stop after my grandpa's call, and upon me getting out, Grandfather opened his door as well.

I looked back, and I saw him standing by the sedan, starting to come after me along the side of the street. We'd stopped in the middle of city traffic, cars honking around us, but my attention was divided, on my phone. I was getting my legal shit together like Royal said. I needed to get my mom completely out of my grandpa's fucking care.

"Knight!"

I turned back, and I saw his hand on his chest, no longer able to come after me. Nigel hurried to him, but Grandfather pushed him off him. "I'm fine, Nigel. Knight, come back. Please! You have to understand, son. I did what I thought was best for you!"

Well, his best wasn't mine, his best put me in a category of a lot of shit I tried so fucking hard not to be. Greer was right about something else in the end. I'd failed my father…

But I'd failed my mom worse.

CHAPTER
TWENTY-THREE

Greer

I sat on the kitchen counter at Mom and Ben's house, peering on while Mom cooked dinner for Ben and me. We weren't able to do any of our takeout nights recently due to both Ben and her being out of work, and though they did both get severance pay, it'd only last so long. Ben was currently out on interviews now for police work in other counties. Either way, we'd all probably have to move after term completed for me. My housing package throughout the rest of the year wouldn't mean much if I couldn't pay for school, and though I'd looked into scholarships and grants, those wouldn't be divvied out until the next academic year. Knight and his bull-shit had screwed both my family and me again, and not only had I let him do it, I'd been the reason why. He'd been mad at me, me and my meddling that probably hadn't even been valid. He knew his mom's situation far greater than I did, so what gall did I have to actually get involved? Not much, and a career in anything that currently involved a degree seemed to be pretty damn far out of reach these days.

Mom frowned at me from the skillet, and because I knew she didn't like when I sat on the counter, I got off, lounging a hip against the kitchen counter instead to shuck corn. I tossed the husk in the trash. "This is a mess. You can't fight this?"

I'd more than explained how screwed up it'd been to not only fire them both, but on such late notice. They'd had jobs one day, then the next—gone, and that was completely fucked. The university had no right do that.

"Tides change, bug. You move with them or get crushed by the waves." Mom pressed the three burgers with her spatula, way too calm about Ben's and her current situation. She shook her head. "What's done is done."

I wanted her to fight for herself, *do something*, but what right did I have to demand that? I'd gotten them both fired in the first place, something I'd kept close to the cuff due to nothing but my own guilt. Even still, the fact couldn't be denied that the Reeds felt they were gods when they came to our lives. Had for a decade now. "Knight and his grandfather are assholes."

The university had told Mom and Ben they'd been let go due to budget cuts, but I knew the truth and I did tell him the Reeds had pulled their funding. Mom and Ben, of course, had passed that off, saying there was no direct correlation, but of course, I knew the truth.

Mom tsked. "When will you stop blaming that boy for getting your stepdad and me fired? And what happened? I thought you two…"

Her words drifted off, and *I* swallowed. The moment Knight and his grandpa's role in their firing came out my mouth Mom knew something was up, up between Knight and me…

She'd just been too nice to ask about it.

She'd at least put two and two together that absolutely nothing was going on between Knight Reed and me. At least not anymore.

"It doesn't matter what the Reeds do with their money," Mom continued. "And even if that was the reason, what the university does is on the university. I don't blame the Reeds, and if I could blame them, I wouldn't. It's their money to do with what they wish, and I'd have no right."

How could she stand there and say that? How could she keep defending the Reeds time and time again? I didn't understand—at all. Knight sat at her table, ate her and Ben's food, and still, she wasn't upset.

"That's all a joke."

"What is?"

Fuck, she'd heard me. I'd meant to say it under my breath. I shook my head. "Nothing, Mom."

"No 'nothing, Mom.'" She flipped the burgers, stepping away from the skillet, then wiping her hands on a kitchen towel. "What is a joke?"

"It's just like, the Reeds can do no wrong in your eyes. *Knight* can do no wrong."

"Why would you say that? Is this about all that stuff when you guys were kids?" Sighing, she pulled a veil of her hair out of her face. "That boy is not at fault for me losing my job."

"How so?" I dropped corn in a bowl. "The guy goes crazy, kills a dog at like eleven. I mean, who does that? He's crazy. Even then. Then there's Mr. Reed. He swept what happened under the rug to save face for what his crazy grandson did." I groaned. "He kicked us out, tossed us out on the street, and we lived in our car, Mom!"

"That's not what happened, and yes, we lived in our car but that was not an eleven-year-old boy's fault, and he's not crazy. Don't call him that."

"What else could explain it? Kids don't kill dogs—"

"Well, that kid did for you."

She froze me where I stood with her words. Releasing a breath, she pressed palms to her face, and I pushed off the counter. I frowned. "What do you mean he did for me?"

"Like I said, he did for you." Then reaching over, she lifted my pant leg. "Or did you forget how you got that scar?"

I stared down at the faded bite mark. Of course I hadn't forgotten. I mean, I got bit by a dog. "No, I didn't forget."

Mom let go, sighing. "That boy hunted down that dog and killed it for you. He saw it follow you. Went after it himself with that friend he had. I forget his name."

"Royal Prinze?" My mouth was dry, and Mom nodded.

"Yes, him. Knight heard you screaming. Terrified." Her eyes lifted. "So pardon me if I'm not mad at the boy who saved my daughter. That dog had been an absolute terror in the neighborhood. An absolute terror and clearly, the adults weren't doing anything about it. Mr. Peabody, Knight's neighbor, was a very powerful man too, just like the Reeds, and damn if the city officials would take his dog away from him. Knight ended up doing what no one else could. He took matters into his own hands, even then, and saved you."

I couldn't believe what I was hearing. Knight went after a dog for me? No way. I shook my head. "How do you know he went after it for me specifically?" That dog had chased everyone, not just me, and for all I knew, he and Royal had been trying to save themselves. That dog had chased me for what felt like miles that day.

Mom pulled her hair out of her face again before turning off the burner. "He told his grandfather the whole thing. That he went after that dog for you, and after hearing that, yes, I was let go. Part of the reason was because yeah, the Reeds like as little drama as possible in their lives, but the main one did have to do with you."

"Me?"

She frowned. "His grandson was willing to kill a dog for you, honey bug, so no, I don't blame Mr. Reed. I mean, that's really intense. Like you said, Knight was just a kid, and he did that. Needless to say, it was clear a little Knight Reed obviously cared about you. *Still* cares about you judging by what I saw when we had him over for dinner. I saw him here with you." She smiled. "It's like you were never out of his eye, not for a moment, honey bug. It was all still so very intense. Just like when you guys were kids."

I couldn't breathe, shuddering. She had to have gotten the facts wrong. No way did Knight Reed care about anyone but himself.

"And his grandfather didn't let me go empty-handed," Mom continued. "He provided a handsome final paycheck. I just couldn't get us stable, a job and housing, before the funds ran out. So none of that is the Reeds' fault either. That was me and my irresponsibility."

I palmed my eyes, barely listening at this point, and Mom took my hand.

"I'm sure Knight's not perfect, bug. But really, who is? That boy has really been dealt a shitty deck of cards in life, and his grandfather was no help. He always treated him like a little adult. I joked about it a bit with you and Ben, but really, it was sad every day I saw it. It was like his granddad matured him up just so hard. I mean, I get it. His mom's accident? His dad dying right in front of him before that…"

My lips parted. "What?"

Her gaze found mine, her expression even sadder. "It was obviously before you and I came, but prior to his mom's accident his dad died. Mr. Reed explained everything to me when I was hired so I was in the know when it came to Knight. He had some really rough years before our arrival, acting out, and yes, a little violent. Got in fights all the time at school—"

"What happened, Mom?" I moved in and she peered away.

"It was a riding accident," she said. "Horseback riding. He and his dad went out. His dad got bucked. Horse trampled him. The man broke his neck."

My heart twisted. "In front of him?"

She sighed. "In front of him. Couldn't have been more than eight."

Nine actually. He'd told me his dad died right before his mom went into the coma.

Christ.

Mom squeezed my shoulders, pulling me into her. "It just shows me how lucky I am. We are? I couldn't imagine leaving you by yourself. Especially that young. Your father was a deadbeat, and before Ben, you were all I had. I needed to take care of you."

And I needed to take care of her, my arms pulling around her. She kissed the top of my head, and when she moved to let go, I didn't. She was right, we were lucky.

I mean, how easily could something like this be taken away?

———

Greer

I thought a lot on the bus ride that night on my way back to the dorm, a lot about Knight. I'd had no freaking idea he'd done all that for me. Obviously, just thinking he'd gone crazy.

Chills lining my skin, I sat up as I got closer to my stop. I tugged the cord to be let off a couple blocks from the dorm, the closest I could get on that route. Hitting the ground, I was in a blind stupor as I left the bus and started walking under the street lights to head home. If it was fact what my mom said tonight, that explained a lot, a lot about Knight's character and who he'd obviously become as a man. He was very intense, aggressive to the point of being scary, and though I sympathized with him, he had scared me in the past. Frankly, he was terrifying sometimes, so hot and cold. And now what he'd done recently? Hurting Ben and Mom just to get to me?

I shook my head, all this terribly complicated. He obviously had a lot of pain in his life, but that didn't excuse all the things he'd done since he'd returned to mine. He'd hurt me, repeatedly, and when my phone buzzed on my final block home, I seriously thought I was haunted by a ghost. Knight's name appeared on my phone screen, and I'd just been thinking about him.

Knight: Hey. Where are you?

My heart squeezed. He had no right to ask me where I was, but even still, I decided to answer.

Me: Walking home from the bus stop. Why?

The text pinged quick.

Knight: Are you by yourself?

Me: Yeah. About a block from the dorm. Why?

Knight: What street crossing?

Me: Fifth and Main. Why???

Knight: Don't fucking move. I'm coming—

Grabbed, instantly, and my phone fell as I was shoved against the ground. Two guys were on top of me, one holding down my arms while the other attempted to rip my bag off my arm. They were wearing black masks, dark hoodies and slacks, and the one on my back forced my face into the ground, cutting off a scream. I bucked. "Take it! I don't fucking care. Just get off me!"

They took the bag easily, but I noticed the one on my back didn't get off me. His hand encased my throat, squeezing all air from my lungs. He leaned in. "We'll take something else if you don't mind, sweetness." The one on my back slapped the other against his chest, easily both guys with their sizes. "Who knew we'd be going after such a sweet piece of ass."

The other laughed, my scream cut off again when the guy on my back pushed his knee between my legs. "Relax, sweetness. It won't hurt. *Much*."

The guy on my back started to grab my leg, but the other

held his shoulder. He shook his head. "Bro, we were just paid to mess with her."

"And we are," said who was clearly the leader. He glanced around the area, the world dark, and sickness rose at how incredibly alone I was in this situation. It was just me and these guys, these two who'd obviously intended to hurt me. The guy on my back honed in, smelling starkly of alcohol. "But since no one's around, how about we play with her a little bit."

The other guy curled a finger against my face, obviously agreeing, but while they were debating whatever sick and twisted shit they planned, I was balling my fist.

I twisted beneath the guy on my back, swinging and socking the fucker right in his throat.

He gasped, falling off me and grabbing his windpipe. The other asked him if he was okay, and I grabbed his shoulders, kneeing him in his balls.

He shot off a curse immediately, falling to the ground, and scraping from between the two of them, I got my bearings, getting the fuck out of there. I'd never been so fucking happy for those moves my stepdad cop taught me.

"Fucking get her!"

In turning back to see who said that, I crashed into a wall, immediately embraced by a sturdy set of arms.

"Greer? What the fuck?" Eyes wild, Knight grappled me, pulling me up by the arms. "You okay? Where are those fuckers who came after you?"

He *knew* I'd been attacked? Panicking from a near assault, I couldn't formulate words, but it turned out, I didn't need to. Knight's gaze passed clear over me to the guys who were still reeling from being kicked in the balls and punched in the throat. The assholes were quite literally on their backsides, and seeing that, Knight's eyes twitched wide. He faced me. "Did you do that?"

Fuck yeah, I had. I nodded. "Ben showed me some stuff. He said just in case." And thank God he had.

Knight's hand moved over my face and outlining my mouth, he chuckled. "I've never been more grateful for that fight and mouth."

He let me go after that, told me to stay where I was and call the cops. Before I knew it, he was going over to both of the guys, picking them up by the scruffs of their shirts like they were freakin' toddlers.

One flailed. "Hey, man. What the fuck—"

A jab to the face of one, followed by a boot to the stomach once he hit the ground. After Knight got that one down, he started in on the other, repeated jabs over and over again to the face. "You a big tough guy, huh?" He growled, another hit. "Messing with girls? You want to hit someone? Fucking *hit me*."

No one was getting any hits in, not with Knight repeatedly going back and forth between the two. Upon finding my phone, I called the police and told them what was up quickly. After, I ran over to Knight. "Stop. They're down, okay?"

He wouldn't stop, a blind rage and probably would have continued if not for the sirens. Before I knew it, a few armed officers were getting out of their squad cars, Knight barely able to be peeled away so they could do their jobs. The cops started to go for Knight too until I cut in. "No. It was just those masked guys. Knight was helping me."

I put my hand on his chest, his heart beating a mile a minute inside his mighty chest. Staring at me, he looped an arm around my waist and grabbed hold of my bib overalls, like he needed a hold of me just to stay stable. He didn't let up until both guys were arrested, and even then, it was only to take my hand. He placed it right on mine…

The one on top of his heart.

CHAPTER
TWENTY-FOUR

Knight

After the police settled things down and took our statements, Greer and I went back to her apartment. I refused to let her walk the rest of the way by herself, and to my surprise, she actually invited me upstairs after I walked her.

"Want something to drink?" she asked me, her roommates not in. Though since she texted them right after we got in, I could imagine they'd be here soon. They'd been blowing up her phone with texts even more than her Mom had. Greer called her at the scene, and both her mom and her stepdad had quite reasonably freaked out. The thing had been a fucking mess, but eventually, Greer had been able to talk them both down. They almost came, but Greer told them she had me to walk her back to the dorm, the only reason they let her.

I refused the drink, taking the couch, but noticing me clench and unclench my hand, Greer asked me to spread my fingers.

"It's nothing," I said, but I showed her, my knuckles split

and cracked in several places. The burning in my bones might have told me I'd done more damage than just that, but I didn't fucking care. I wasn't going to any hospital. When it came to doctors these days, needless to say, I had my reservations.

This couldn't be helped considering the situation with my mom, and I watched Greer leave the room, the back of her bib coveralls dirty from when those fuckers had tackled her to the ground. I should go to county lock up myself and finish the job I'd started on those ass wipes who'd attacked her. Thank God she'd been able to hold her own until I got there. She returned to the room with a first aid kit, pulling back her silky blond hair as she got on her knees on the carpet before me. I wanted to touch it, touch her as she pulled rubbing alcohol out of the kit and cotton balls.

She frowned. "Did you know those guys were going to attack me tonight?"

A curse left my lips when she dabbed my knuckles. My jaw moved. "Why would you think that?"

Silence as she touched me with alcohol again, and once clean, she smoothed some ointment on the knuckles. She pressed gauze to my hand after that, wrapping the whole thing with medical tape she tore free with her teeth. She shrugged. "I mean, you texted me right before those guys came."

"So?"

Her frown deepened. "So it's weird. You told me to wait for you, that you were coming like you knew something was going to happen."

More silence as she wrapped my hand, and pride was a real fucking thing. I didn't want to tell her the truth, hell all my truths. But in the end, I guess she deserved it. In fact, she deserved so much more than I'd given her in the past and probably could ever give. I worked my fingers bound with tape. "I was tipped off that a couple of guys were coming after you. Paid to do so by my grandpa."

Her eyebrows jumped. "What?"

How long and fucked up the story was. I sighed, scrubbing my burning fingers through my hair. "My grandpa went to the frat looking for volunteers. Those guys, Garret and Hunter, I knew. They're pieces of shit no one likes and willing to do pretty much anything for a buck and some entertainment for the night. Some of the other guys at the frat obviously knew about the coup since Grandfather poked around asking for someone to mess with you. The guys called me up, let me know about it. Apparently, Garret and Hunter were just supposed to handle you, scare you, but knowing those fuckers, I highly doubt that's all they'd stop at."

Absolute horror behind Greer's eyes, her swallow hard. "Why would your grandpa do that? Why would he send people after me?"

And so the truth came out, all of it. Still livid, my body visibly shook. "Because you were right. You were right about fucking everything." I breathed harshly into my hands, and Greer joined me on the couch.

"Right?" She touched my shoulder, and I faced her.

"My grandpa was keeping my mom in that coma," I said, her mouth parting. "He was keeping her asleep and has been for twelve years. She woke up eight days after her accident, Greer. Eight fucking days."

"What the fuck?"

Nodding, I stared away. "He said she was trying to take me away from him after my dad died, that he was trying to protect me because my mom was a whore. I guess my dad married an escort and Gramps didn't like that. He didn't think she could be a parent after my dad died."

She covered her face with her hands, gasping. "Oh, Knight."

"I've spent the last few days just trying to get her out of his care, but he hasn't made it easy. There's all this red tape I didn't know about, legal shit, and I'm trying to work my way through it, but she's still in that goddamn nursing home. He has power of attorney over her and her care." I didn't know if I'd ever get her out, if I could save her or even if she could be saved. Now that my grandpa knew that *I knew*, he may kill her. Finish the job he'd started before I got a chance to get her. I looked at Greer. "When I found out about all this, I mentioned your name. It fucking slipped about you being right about all this, and though my grandpa obviously didn't remember you when he'd seen you those handful of times, he asked around. He found out you went to Pembroke. He found out you came with me to the nursing home. Your name was on the damn sign-in sheet."

She shook beside me, staring off, and her lips trembled as she looked at me. "So he sent someone after me?"

"Probably because in his sick, fucked up way, he believed he was protecting me. Protecting me from you and all the chaos you bring." I covered my face. "Thank God he hadn't found out you'd been there that night with Bryce. A loose end he'd have to shut down."

Because he would have wiped her way, done so just to prove a point. That Greer Michaelson was trouble, trouble I needed to stay away from. True, chaos accompanied her whenever she seemed to be in my life, but that wasn't her fault. She was a victim, always the victim, and I'd made that so fucking worse for her in the past it made me sick. I'd hurt her. Hurt her so many times and still continued to do it. My grandpa just shy of put a hit out on her head tonight, and if she hadn't been able to hold her own…

I didn't even want to think about it, maddened to the point of insanity. Small hands made their way around my bicep, tugging at me, and I realized how clamped up I was.

She touched my face. "He's why you threatened me." That realization she discovered now too, cringing with damp eyes.

"Oh my God, Knight."

I brought chaos into this girl's life, none of it deserved. I shook my head. "I fucked up, Greer. I fucked up, and I hurt you."

"No—"

I removed her hands. "I fucking did, and I don't even have the words. All that terrible shit I did to you…"

Her hands touched me again, and I didn't fucking deserve it, none of this. She should run the far fuck away, who I was a monster just like every other demon that plagued the town I came from. I could add my grandpa to that list now, a true devil in sheep's clothing. He may have had his own reasons, but the end far from hell justified the means. He was just as cruel, just as sick as everyone else.

Greer's fingers curled against my jaw, and I actually shuddered, taking her hand. I kissed it. "I'm so fucking sorry."

"Just stop. Stop, okay? Look at me."

I did, cringing. "How can you even look at me right now?" Because she was and not in the terror she should. There was so much sympathy in her eyes, empathy even. She was being understanding when she fucking shouldn't.

She let go of me after that, but only to jerk her pant leg above her ankle. On her pale skin was a scar, the gruesome remains of a bite mark in a location I was well aware of. Old Man Peabody's dog had bitten her there, another way I'd failed her. I let her get fucking bitten that day. I should have taken care of that dog sooner.

"I have to admit," she said, chewing her lip a little. "Back then, I didn't understand. It's still hard for me." She let go and touched my jaw. "But now, I *need* to."

Her mouth touched mine, and I couldn't breathe, my arm gripping around her and bringing her close. She shouldn't let me kiss her. She shouldn't let me have any of this, but I pulled her into my lap, teasing her mouth open with my tongue.

She sighed as her arms fell around me, her heat giving my

body life. My phone rang, and I wanted to ignore it, to have this and not let her go, but I knew I couldn't.

I eased her away. "It might be my lawyers about my mom," I said, pulling it out. "They're trying to get me through all this red tape with my grandpa."

They were trying to get me *her*, and not only did Greer understand that, she waited for me to look at my phone. I saw Nigel, my grandpa's driver, and was instantly livid. My nostril's flared.

Greer frowned. "Who is it?"

"My grandpa's driver," I said before taking a breath and swiping to take the call. "Nigel, you can tell my grandpa—"

"I'm at the hospital with him, sir."

I sat up. "Hospital?"

Greer looked at me, frowning again. She moved closer, but I didn't move, the phone firmly planted against my ear.

"Yes, sir," Nigel continued, his voice gruff, strained. "And I wish I could bring you better news, but…"

I heard the pumping blood in my ears, my eyes staring at nothing but everything as I waited for him to speak. He did, and I just about allowed the phone to leave my hand.

"You know how his heart was," he continued, emotion in the man's voice. "I got him here quick, sir, but… it was just too late."

"Knight, what's going on?"

I faced Greer, Nigel still speaking to me. I could say nothing to her. I could say nothing to him. He was telling me my grandpa had died.

He was telling me my grandpa had had a heart attack.

CHAPTER
TWENTY-FIVE

Greer

Life had a way of handing us things beyond our control sometimes, and in Knight's case, that ended up being what allowed Knight's mom to both be taken and returned to him in the end. A lot of that red tape his grandpa put him through to keep his mom away ended up dissolving, though tragically considering the circumstances. His grandpa had fought him to the end, and that may have been the very thing that had triggered his heart attack, something Knight not only dealt with but had been the bigger person in the end. He handled all the arrangements, was there for his grandpa even in death and even with divided attention. His mom was priority now that he'd finally gained power of attorney over her, but even still, he gave his grandpa a proper send off.

Like I said, way bigger than probably most would have been.

His grandpa's "protection" had been under the form of pain and suffering, a heavy hand, and Knight not only rose above it, but did all he could to correct. His mom was out of that nursing home the next day, flown up state for the best care and *his* doctors. He took care of her, was by her side even while balancing school and his grandpa's funeral. He got everything done, and when she ultimately woke up, came back from a twelve-year coma, he was by her bedside again. She couldn't speak, of course. It wasn't like in the movies where someone got up, love in their eyes as they embraced the family who'd long been waiting for their return. The process was tragically slow, an eye blink, some finger movement, and mumbled words. The doctors said it'd take weeks, months, or maybe even years of therapy, and she still may not return to who she used to be. But even still, Knight didn't give up hope. Even still, he was there.

And I was too.

I was at lunch when I got Knight's text that day and dropped everything the minute I saw it. It said three words.

Knight: She's coming home.

I'd known this was a possibility today since he'd gone to see her, and after telling him how excited I was for him, he'd said he'd send a car to pick me up after my last class. He wanted me there, there with him when his mom returned home. Needless to say, I was more than excited and honored that he trusted me enough to be there for him. Things with his mom had been tumultuous to say the least, *slow*, but I'd been there. I'd been there too when she'd first opened her eyes, by his side and taking in the world. His mom hadn't recognized him, of course, and from what I understood, he hadn't told her. Everything was so new for her, still very slow. Knight and her doctors were taking things day by day, but still, she must have been doing well enough in her therapy for them to green-light her return home. This was a really happy day, and I was so excited for him.

Knight sent a town car to come get me after my final class of the day, and after going back to my dorm to get an overnight bag, I climbed in for my ride. My roommates wished me luck before. They all knew the situation and I was happy for their support. Especially Haley who not only stepped back from the situation with Knight but had shared the most support. I had such good friends and roommates and knew how lucky I was.

In the town car, I gazed out onto the road. I was going back to Maywood Heights today, Knight's hometown and where his grandpa's estate was. The estate had been in their family for generations, a place I once lived too for a short time. I was kind of nervous to be going back there, but the circumstances were way different than those final days when his grandpa had fired my mom. I knew all the facts now, the background, and was not only overwhelmed by it but by who Knight was. He'd been protecting me since we were kids, and I couldn't help smiling when I thought about my boyfriend.

Oh, yeah. That was new as well, so many things changing. Through all this, Knight and I came back to each other, so different from how we'd both begun. Even when we'd been kids. He was so much gentler now, his experience with his mom only helping.

I texted him during the duration of the ride to Maywood Heights, asking him for updates. He couldn't give me much, just that she was home and laying down but simply hearing from him made my heart soar.

Knight: I'm so glad you're coming. You don't even know.

So different than how he was, but then again. I think I was different too. I was stronger, changed in the best way. I texted Knight how close I was, and as we pulled past that welcome sign greeting me into the town of Maywood Heights, I got a buzz in my pocket from Mom.

Mom: Wish Knight and his mom luck for us. Ben and I are thinking about you both. Love you!

Mom and Ben, of course, knew everything too, and once more, Mom was that supportive rock I loved. Knight corrected everything with them, speaking to the school personally about their jobs. I didn't know exactly what all the talks entailed, but Mom and Ben had their jobs back within hours of him reaching out. Knight even apologized to them personally, profusely. Once more, my mom hadn't shown any feelings of anger or resentment. She was just so kind spirited, always had been. As an extra special apology, Knight sent both Mom and Ben off on a second honeymoon, a cruise to the Caribbean which was where they were currently now. I kept getting pictures and had been too jealous since I was still at school and forced to live vicariously through them and their Facebook photos.

Me: Thank you. I'll pass that along. Not sure what state his mom is in today, but I'm hopeful.

Mom: We are too. That boy deserves that. He needs his mama.

I'd especially agree if she was anything at all remotely like mine. She'd been there for me my whole life, my rock.

I told them to enjoy the rest of their time on their vacation and after giving me their love, I noticed the car slowing down.

"We're coming up on Reed Manor, miss," the driver said, stealing my attention.

Reed Manor, a distant memory in my thoughts, and I leaned forward, peering through the tinted window. Steel gates opened to the wide property of a well-trimmed lawn, rose bushes lining the path toward an exquisite fountain. Just behind was the grand estate Reed Manor and still as beautiful as I remembered as a child. A gray brick castle, Knight's property sat tucked behind a sea of well-trimmed hedges and flower boxes filled with elegant daisies. The place was literally like a castle out of a storybook, and I spent lots of time hiding in as many places I could find. It'd been fun for me, like a little adventure of my own to explore.

Knight's driver pulled us up to the doors, and after letting me out, I told him I'd take my own bag to the door. Knight wanted me to stay for the weekend, and since things with classes were going so well, I hadn't had a problem with that.

I wheeled my bag up to the door and started to knock before it was pulled open, a woman in a white coat and an elegant grin behind it.

"Greer, welcome. Knight and his mom are upstairs. I'll take you to both of them."

Recognizing the woman as Dr. Chopra, one of the doctors caring for Knight's mom, I thanked her and followed. From what I understood, she'd be overseeing his mom for around-the-clock care now that she was home and had been very nice in the times I'd seen her. It'd been a lot. I'd been a frequent visitor during his mom's rehabilitation process and at Knight's side whenever I could be.

I kept pace with the doctor, my bag taken by one of the maids of the house. I recognized her too, an older woman who still worked here after my mom and I had left. She said she'd leave it in my room and would show it to me after my visit with the master of the house.

The master of the house turned out to be upstairs, inside a room facing the sun. Light literally bled upon my shoes once Dr. Chopra opened the door, and the first thing I noticed after the sun was Knight and his mom. It was basically drowning them in it, Knight sitting in an easy chair with his hands folded. He was leaning forward, staring at a woman in bed hooked up to many lines.

"Go ahead," Dr. Chopra whispered, closing the door behind me when I went inside. I honestly didn't want to disrupt the peace of this room, but the moment the door closed, dark eyes shifted my way, a gorgeous guy rising from his chair.

"Dove," fell from Knight's lips as he crossed the room to me, hard and perfect muscle gripping me into an embrace. He basically picked me up off my feet, my weight nothing for him. "I'm so happy you're here."

He kissed me after that, hands in my hair and everything as he pushed it out of my face.

"Your drive okay?" he asked, easing a heavy arm around me, and I nodded, so happy to see him too. The moments I wasn't with him, I found it hard to breathe, how much really had changed. I think I found myself falling in love with this boy, so hard and damn fast.

I smiled. "I did. How's she doing?"

Panning, I studied the woman so gorgeous beneath silk sheets. She was hooked up to a lot of monitors, but nothing like when she'd been at the hospital. She actually looked at peace here, her long, dark hair resting on her shoulders.

A smile and Knight tugged me over to her with him. We sat down together by her bedside, his hand still in mine, but I couldn't help noticing the worry that twisted his brow. This was a recurring expression during this whole process as well.

"She's sleeping now. Just sleeping." Leaning forward again, he rubbed my hand between his. "I know it's dumb, but I can't stop looking at her. I think a part of me is scared she won't wake up again."

He said this shyly like he was ashamed when he shouldn't be. I mean, the woman had been in a coma for more than half his life. "That's not dumb. It's normal. I'd be worried too, but I don't think you have to be. You have the best doctors now."

"I know, but still." His fingers lazily warmed mine again. "I'm just scared, dove. And not just about that."

"About what then?"

His tongue dampened his lips before he faced me. "Say she does come back."

"She will."

He smiled. "Say she does and I'm not who she wants me to be. That I'm… I don't know. A letdown or something." He shook his head before looking at her. "I'd hate that. I've done so many stupid things."

He had, but that was what made us human. I touched his

jaw, and with it, I got his eyes. "You're her son, and though I'm not a parent, something tells me there's little you could do where she'd want nothing to do with you. Where you'd disappoint her? Knight, she loves you…"

"Knight?"

The voice had been faint when I heard it, soft, but the moment I did, chills lined my skin. They'd been good chills, ones that had me gripping Knight's hand. I didn't even have to ask if he'd heard his name as well.

Immediately, his eyes darted over to his mom, fastening on her gaze. She stared right at us, *at him*, and her fingers lifted from the sheets. "Knight…"

He rose, instantly taking her hand, and immediately, I got up, calling for Dr. Chopra. His mom didn't do this, call for him or anyone. Her speech was usually pretty mumbled, like she was out of it most of the time, but she definitely wasn't now. She called specifically for Knight, wanting his hand.

"Mom." He warmed hers between his, focusing on nothing but her, and my eyes watered, his too as he smiled at her. "Yeah, Mom. It's me. Knight. Your son."

"Knight," she whispered again, and he touched her cheek. Her lips lifted, a soft smile forming them. "So big."

Laughter, emotion-lined as he nodded at her. "I am, but it's me. I swear it is."

He kissed her hand, closing his eyes, and I couldn't breathe, watching the two of them together. It took me a while to realize Dr. Chopra and her team had arrived but, like me, stayed frozen in place. At the door, they watched on, studying the scene with smiles like I was. They refused to break this moment, and neither would I…

A mother who finally returned to her son.

EPILOGUE

Knight

"Knight? Would you stay off your fucking phone already! We're supposed to be going to a party. Jesus."

I grumbled at the peanut gallery in the front seat, my buddy's fiancee never laying off. December had been bugging the shit out of me for pretty much the entire car ride to Woodcreek University for being on my phone.

Growling from the back seat, I put my phone away, then slung it over the shoulders of my little dove. Greer, *my girlfriend*, knew why I needed to be on my phone and wasn't giving me a hard time. I jerked my chin at December. "Mind your own business. I need to know what's going on with my mom."

Hence all the text messaging. Dr. Chopra received them on her behalf since not only were smart phones not really a thing yet when my mom went into a coma, she still wasn't in a place to be trying to text anyone. Phone calls were still hard for her even, but with her therapy over the last couple months she'd been getting better. I liked to not have to deal with any of that, though, and just be with her tonight.

December turned in her seat, my buddy Royal driving right next to her. December smiled. "We know. That's why you're getting away for the weekend with us."

"She's just trying to help, man." Royal made eye contact through the rearview mirror, his fingers lacing with December's. "We all are. We just want to give you a weekend. Something where you can just relax."

I didn't want to relax, but I knew they were right. Since my mom had woken up, she'd been my whole life. Well, her and Greer. I had so much catching up to do with my mom. We'd lost twelve goddamn years.

Hugging up under me, Greer had obviously agreed with the decision to get me out of the manor. She'd nudged me to get on the road with December and Royal to go visit our buddy LJ at his university, and though I'd listened to her, it'd been my mom to ultimately let me be okay with the decision to take a weekend away from her. She'd said I'd been stressing over her too much as well.

She had actually said that.

She'd come a long way in so little time, something that was such a relief for me. All that my grandpa had done... there might just be some light on the end of it. I wasn't sure if that was possible when in the thick of it. And despite what my grandpa's passing had allowed, my mom and me to come back together, I was far from happy with how it'd come to pass. I loved my grandpa. He had raised me.

I just didn't love a lot of the things he'd done.

I was seeing someone about all that too, ways to deal with my anger. I really believed it was helping, and the fact that Mom was so positive after all that had happened, despite finding out what my grandpa had done to her, kept my spirits high too. If she could be okay, at peace with the years she'd lost and the time away from me, who was I not to do the same? I had a pretty kickass Mom, and I couldn't wait to see what life would bring us. I hoped to even have a fraction of what Greer and her mom had. They were really close, and Greer's mom and Ben had even come to see mine. They had all stayed with Mom and me over holiday break at the manor.

Greer played with my fingers, grinning. "You know you don't have to worry about her, right? Your mom?" She shook me. "She'll be fine. She's freaking Superwoman."

She was right, of course. Mom had been awake for nearly three months now, and not only was she talking and having full conversations, she was out of her bed. She was still mostly confined to her wheelchair, but with her continued physical therapy, her doctors seemed very hopeful about her walking and getting to be herself again.

Because I listened to my girlfriend, I kissed her, then rolled my eyes at Royal and his girl through the mirror.

Royal smirked in response and pulled his arm around December. Things were gratefully quiet the rest of the way up to Woodcreek-U. Our buddy LJ was having a weekend bash. Fuck, when wasn't he having parties at the Ivy League he attended? He'd been bugging Royal and me to come up for months and even worse when he came back home for Christmas break. The guys, Royal, LJ, along with our other friend Jax, have all been bugging me to get out more lately, but it was only after Greer and my mom had insisted that I decided to give in and make the car trip happen. I didn't listen to many people, but I did listen to the women in my life, my light in the dark.

Greer had been with me this whole fucking time, around through my mom's therapy, her slow process of recovery, and even my grandpa's funeral. She had showed up by my side through it all, pain or good times... didn't matter. She was there, which was more than I had been for her in the past. She didn't have to be around for me. She didn't have to show up, but she did. I'd spend a lifetime trying to make that up to her.

I hoped, ultimately, that was what was in the cards for us.

Those thoughts for another day, I relaxed with my girl, Royal's Audi slushing through January ice. Eventually, we all pulled up to LJ's place, and I actually whistled at the sight of the modern-style home basically the size of my frat. The place was fucking lit, huge-ass windows that surrounded the whole place and with enough people and strobe lights inside to let us know the party was ongoing.

"Things must be going all right for him," I told Royal when we got out, the guy eyeing me. LJ, unlike Royal, Jax, and me, didn't really come from money. In fact, he'd been dirt poor when we knew him and came to college on a full-ride scholarship.

The guys and I had been let in on a little bit of what LJ had been doing since he went away for school. From what we knew, he'd started promoting parties, small stuff that led to… bigger stuff, but at the end of the day, that was his business. We were bros, family, and we'd support him in whatever he chose to do.

Royal tugged December over, and I did the same with Greer, warming her shoulders in the chill as we fought our way through the crowds. This place was on the level, and barely inside the door, we found LJ. The tall motherfucker shot above the heads of everyone else in the room, his arm around our other buddy Jax, who was flailing his arms like a monkey in front of some girls. Jax was obviously trying to impress them, being an idiot like he was always.

"Nice to see not much has changed." Royal edged over, then cupped his mouth to holler at the pair. His voice boomed above the crowd, getting the attention of our boys, and as they waved us over, I realized how much I'd truly missed my brothers. Our brotherhood went beyond our time in the Court and was way thicker than what college and a few hundred miles could put between us. We were family, and after

greeting the boys and they said hello to December, I introduced the guys to my girl.

"This is my little dove." I swiped a finger beneath her
chin, that snow-white hair pushed up and showcasing that
sexy-as-fuck neck of hers. I'd gotten a handful of her delicate
throat while I pounded into her just this morning, my cock
heavy and hard at just the thought of it. Unable to help
myself, I bent, touching a kiss to that soft skin, and she
shoved at my chest.

"Knight." She rolled her eyes, but she was a terrible
fucking liar. So much heat lined her gaze the moment I
touched her neck, straight fire in her blue eyes.

I tugged her over. "Don't bother fighting it, baby. We're
inevitable."

A promise in my voice as I looked at her, those baby blues
electrifying. December basically made a gagging nose, and
the rest of the guys hit me on my arm.

LJ smirked. "Nice to meet you…"

"Greer," she said, forcing distance between us again with
a smile. Of course the guys knew her name. They knew all
about her, but I assumed LJ was just being polite.

He raised a beer to her, Jax too after he said hello. LJ
grinned. "Nice to see someone managed to tame this big oaf."

"Like you should fucking talk." I gazed around, my arm
falling to settle on Greer's hips. "I don't see you with anyone
in this big-ass house."

LJ rolled his eyes before bringing his beer to his lips. After
taking a long swig, he smiled at Greer. "Nice meeting you,
Greer. My house is your house. Just don't let the ass trash it."

I growled, but Greer had been able to hold me back. Good
thing for him too. Greer and I didn't chat with the others long
before deciding to section off and mingle around the house. I
could tell right away Greer was impressed by LJ's digs. Fuck,
even I was. The frat house was pretty kickass, but this was
fucking killer. My buddy definitely was living it up, and as

Greer and I explored the house, I got a buzz from my phone. It followed a few, something I had to check, of course, but even as I juggled my life at home with what I was doing here, Greer didn't complain. In fact, she waited for me during each time I took to text back, her drink in her hand and a smile on her face.

I shot off a quick text to Dr. Chopra, thanking her for letting me know my mom was asleep before pulling Greer over to the wall with me. I got a handful of her sweater, pulling her close. "Have I ever told you how I don't fucking deserve you?"

Because I didn't, not at all, and though I think both of us knew that, she was here anyway. She was *patient* with me anyway. I wasn't easy to get along with, something I knew. Greer balanced all my rough edges, perfect for all my prickly thorns, and though I knew I didn't deserve her, fuck if I was ever letting her go.

To my surprise, she took my hand, tugging me to go with her. We ended up in one of the bedrooms, and when she dropped to her knees, I nearly said *fuck me*.

Fuck me for ever being able to be with a girl like this, setting her drink down before going for my fly. She pulled my cock right out of my pants, knowing how to do this all too well as I'd let her have a lot of practice.

She'd been bold getting on her knees tonight, hot when she felt me up, then put those perfect fuckable lips around me.

Growling, I slammed my hand against the closed door, Greer's head bobbing as she worked my balls and took me deep into her throat. She'd gotten so fucking good at this it was ridiculous.

"Fuck, Greer," I gritted, gripping my fingers into her hair. Holding her to me, she gagged and I nearly came right down her throat. "Don't fucking do that."

My dick fell out of her mouth with a pop. "Do what?" she

asked, her smile coy as she opened her mouth again. She teased my dick with her tongue, starting to pull me into her perfect mouth again, but I got hold of the back of her neck, returning her to her feet.

"LJ's going to kill me," I told her, working that sweater off her perfect tits. Her nipples beaded right through her bra, and I pinched one, grinning at the soft moan she made. I kissed her neck. "For fucking you in here."

I was about ninety percent sure this was my buddy's bedroom. For starters, it was frickin' huge, a bed half the size of the room. It was the type of room I'd definitely choose as my own, but I guess I had the decency not to fuck her on his bed. Hell, who was I kidding…

We definitely weren't going to be making it to the bed.

Tugging Greer's hair free, I got a hand full of it, using it to tug her around and press her tits against the door. I undid her bra, throwing the thing across the room before undoing her jeans.

"Knight…"

The last thing she said before I jerked her head back and took her mouth from above, tasting myself on her lips while I drove my tongue between them. I needed both hands to tweak and tug her sensitive nipples, letting go of her hair to work them between her and the door. I ground my hips against her jean-covered ass, that perfect peach of hers ramming back into me.

"Just fuck me already," she cried, so needy. What had I done to my little virgin? She tired me out most days.

"Do you want me?" I ran my tongue down her spine, pushing both her jeans and underwear down. Her beautiful ass needed a bite, and I sunk my teeth into her left cheek, making her call out.

"Don't tease me." She burned against me, pressing her peach against my mouth. Dipping my finger in her heat, I used it to slide back to her ass, probing it. I hadn't had my dick inside her yet, but we had been using toys.

"You want me to take you back here?" I moved my finger in and out, my digit going deeper and deeper until she had me past the second knuckle. She moaned, giving me her answer, and I stood, grinning. "Only since you asked so nicely."

I got my jeans further down my hips, clean so no need for the condom. I didn't even bring condoms around with me anymore anyway since Greer got on birth control.

Getting a firm hold of her hips, I tugged her up, being gentle as I eased my cock inside her tiny hole. And I mean *eased*, her virgin ass so fucking tight.

"Knight, fuck." She reached back, holding my hip and the cry in her voice froze me where I stood. All this might have been too much for her, but when she worked my hips, I knew she was wanting more.

"Let me know if it doesn't feel good," I coached. I would stop, God fucking help me. I didn't want to hurt her, but shit, if her ass didn't feel good around my dick. Like heaven gracing the earth. Growling, I tugged her earlobe into my mouth, sucking it.

"It feels good." She moaned, grabbing the back of my head. "So good. Don't stop."

All I needed to keep going, working my hips until my thighs slapped against her. I roared as I took her hands and pinned them against the wall. Going as deep as I could, I took us both toward the brink.

"This isn't going to last long," I groaned, taking her off the wall and bending her over a chair. I got better access this way, and when she reached back and gripped her fingernails into my thighs, I was done.

I spilled like a fucking teenager inside her, shuddering while I leaned my weight on her. She stayed positioned there and had the nerve to smile at me after I pulled out and tugged her up.

"Already?" she asked, basically repeating words I'd said to her once upon a time. She needed to give me a break. I hadn't had a girl's ass since well before her. Most girls I'd been with weren't into it.

Apparently, she wasn't most girls.

"I'm going to punish that mouth," I said, teasing her before reaching my fingers between us. I planned to take her over the edge too, strumming her clit while I ground her up against the wall.

She shuddered around me and her hands fell to my shoulders when I got on my knees. I tugged one of her legs over my back, but then I was between her legs, eating her out and munching on her sweet pussy.

"Knight, oh my God." She actually covered her face, like it was all too much before curling her fingers into my back. Grinding against my face, she bunched my shirt in her hands, basically ripping it at the seams she tugged so hard.

"I love you, Greer," I said, every sweet taste of her essence drowning me in that love. I hadn't said that to a girl before, not unless they were family and barely at all in the years my mom was in the coma. Love was hard for me, easily taken away by situation and circumstances. It wasn't easy to open myself to that…

But fuck if it hadn't always been that way with her.

She ran her fingers through my hair as I fucked her with my mouth, holding me close.

"I love you too," she breathed, her body quivering above me. I had a feeling she loved me too. Hell, might have even been able to say it before me even though she hadn't. But despite me knowing, it wasn't the same as hearing it. That someone like her could actually love someone like me… someone so hard and jagged. But then here she was.

She came down just as hard as me, her sweet taste flowing

into my mouth, and I was there for every drop. I didn't want it to end. She was mine, *mine*, but eventually, I did stand, cradling her face.

"Say it again." I wanted to hear her say it, her smile wide.

She touched my chest. "You first."

Chuckling, I bit her lip, pulling both part. "I love you, dove."

"And I love you," she said, wrapping her arms around me when I picked her up. I held her close, and I might just have to have my friend kill me.

I couldn't guarantee I wouldn't fuck the girl I loved into an oblivion on his bed.

Thank you so much for checking out BRUTAL HEIR (Court University 1)! You can get the next book in the Court University saga, KINGPIN, on Amazon.

Did you know there's a website dedicated to all things Court University? There is and it features exclusive content you can't get anywhere else! The website exclusives include playlists, graphics, character bios/photos, and so much more!

Want access to the website? Simply subscribe to my newsletter! There, you'll get new release news from me and a link to the newsletter exclusive Court University website. What are you waiting for? Get access today! =^)

Website access: https://bit.ly/3rf0wha

Knight's story as well as the rest of the boys from the Court University saga began in Court High! Check out their beginnings in THEY THE PRETTY STARS! Read on for a teaser =)

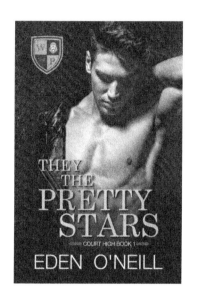

Blurb:

In Maywood Heights, stars burn bright. They fall even harder.

They call them the Court, an elite boys club who rule Windsor Preparatory Academy like gods among men. And, of course, they're led by Hercules himself.

Royal Prinze--yes, that's actually his name--walks around both the school and the town like he owns them. His affiliation to the prestigious Court only gives him more clout. These boys do anything they want. They take anything they want, and they f*ck anything they want... in that order.

Then there's me.

I came to Maywood Heights to live with my virtually indifferent father because my sister went AWOL. She chose to stay with him after our parents' divorce when we were kids, and I haven't seen or heard from her since summer began. The last thing I imagined when enrolling at her school was that she'd be connected to a group like the Court, and boys like Royal. She's nothing like them and so much better than Royal and his elitist attitude...

So, why then are they saying he's her best friend?

Warning: This enemies-to-lovers, high school romance contains some dark themes and light bullying. The book is not a standalone and is book one in a four-part series of full-length novels. Royal Prinze is the only hero of this tale... good luck getting him to share.

One

The air tasted stale here, tasted cold. It wasn't like California. It wasn't like home. Contrary to popular belief, my name being December didn't automatically adjust me to the colder-than-balls Midwestern chill.

I'm going to die when fucking winter hits.

I groaned, seriously questioning my sister's sanity. She'd somehow managed to live here most of her whole life.

You need to get up.

I closed my eyes instead, delaying the inevitable and my father, who no doubt was moving around downstairs. I hadn't heard the door click shut yet, my room directly above.

You need to get up. Get up, Em.

My sister's voice haunted as I pulled myself from warm sheets. They'd been the words she said to me when she left me, left me to move halfway across the country to live with our dad. She left with him after our mom passed, cancer a son of a bitch. I stayed in Cali because that's where we all had lived, our aunt taking me in to live with her. I'd been eight and Paige had been nine, and I didn't need any more damn changes in my life at the time, which had been the reason I stayed. Paige hadn't, though, and it'd been the first time she left me.

This last summer was the second.

I dragged my head up, working my shoulders in an attempt to work the kinks out from an unfamiliar bed. Dad had given me the pick of the house, but I still hadn't gotten used to the sleeping situation yet. With a lazy reach, I grabbed my phone, pressing a button to check for texts. As predicted, Aunt Celeste had checked in on me.

Aunt Celeste: Just wanted to wish you luck on your first day. Let me know if you hear any changes about your sister, but I don't want you to get your hopes up.

As I heard all this before I left, I simply texted back, *I'll be cool and thanks. I will.*

After doing a quick scan of my social media accounts, I stood to hard and creaking floorboards. Aunt Celeste's and my place never creaked, never any give on cheap tiles and dingy carpet. It always worked for us, and lights always stayed on, my stomach fed. Bearing cold creaks with naked feet, I stretched and moved into the bathroom.

Yeah, I have my own bathroom… never getting used to that.

I checked more social media inside, then peeled myself

away long enough to get washed up for my first day at a new school in the middle of a term. I supposed that decision had ultimately been mine, but not made because I actually wanted to uproot myself from my aunt, my friends, and everything I loved about my life. If I had things my way, I'd be back in LA on a bus to *my own* school with a Pop-Tart in my hand.

Paige saw fit to ruin all that.

My older sister better be okay because, if she wasn't, I wouldn't be—this I knew and the reason I made myself put some clothes on and trek downstairs in a house familiar to her and not to me. When Dad had been offered a job that took him *almost* as far away as he could possibly get from our old lives and Paige chose to live with him, I'd been pretty damn shattered for a long time. Paige and I had been more than sisters. We were friends, so yeah, I'd been hella hurt. In the end, I'd been a big girl and eventually gotten over it. There were more opportunities for her with our dad and I got that. She got stuff here with Dad, cars and fancy schools like the one I got to go to today.

"You miss your uniform or something?"

It also got her dad, Dad's eye, and consequently, his scrutiny. I'd naively hoped he'd take his breakfast in the actual nook designated for that. He had all week since I arrived.

My presence known, I eased into the kitchen, my dad taking inventory of my acid-washed jean shorts and oversize top. He snapped his paper over the breakfast bar. "I had Rosanna leave it out for you."

The academy uniform I missed, but probably because she'd placed it in my closet and not out in the open. Rosanna was his housekeeper, and I'd been told if I needed anything to go to her—anything to avoid actually dealing with me.

I wet my lips. "She probably put it in the closet or something. I'll change after breakfast."

His look was dismissive, the same eyes I had with their

deep brown and far less passion for life than he had when he'd been with Mom. My dad had always been a bit of a hard-ass, but when Mom passed, the switch went into overdrive. He didn't deal with any type of emotions. He just worked, all that easier than other things. When Mom died, it gave him an excuse to fall into the rich and opulent life he'd traded for, basically, my hippy mom. She'd been into herbs and crystals where he'd been into stocks and the sports section. Those stocks and his background in banking got him this big-ass house and a fancy job that allowed him to wear those suits he wore at the breakfast table. Most would say I probably took my looks from my dad, straight dark hair, long nose with a button tip, and curved chin. I got my hips from my mom, though, and poor Paige, she'd gotten the crap end of the stick when it came to that. She was nearly as flat-chested as our dad, but she had been skinny, though. So I guess she got that.

Trying to keep the interactions with my dad quick, I headed toward the pantry to get the Pop-Tarts I brought over with me.

"Don't bother with those," he said right as I touched the box. "I'm having Rosanna toss them all out. You don't need all that sugary crap."

My jaw working, I got off my tiptoes and returned my feet to the floor. "What am I supposed to eat?"

"I had Rosanna make you a green smoothie and some eggs. You live with me, you're going to do some changes."

My peripheral caught the foreign drink on the counter, green and no doubt filled with things that'd make me gag this morning. The thing that definitely would make me gag was next to them, though: the eggs under the glass dome filled with steam.

I gripped the counter, turning. "I told you I'm a vegan, Dad. Have been for three years." As he tended to listen to every other word, I supposed he missed that.

He moved the paper. "You mean to tell me Pop-Tarts are vegan?"

"Those kind are, yeah."

"Well, you're not eating them, and I thought vegans were supposed to be healthy. I swear to God, you and your sister and these alternative lifestyles."

By "alternative lifestyle," he meant my sister's sexuality, something he clearly still hadn't dealt with and my sister came out in middle school. Dad was old school amongst other things and always, *always* sought for perfection. That perfection had been my sister's downfall, and I was sure the reason she left. Dad directed a finger. "Drink the smoothie. You'll be all right until lunch."

I supposed, if he had it his way, I wouldn't eat at all, just so he wouldn't have to know about my existence. I'd been acting as his little dark cloud on the West Coast for years now, his secret daughter he hadn't had to deal with. Maybe if he had, I wouldn't have had to be a secret.

And Paige wouldn't have really left to protect me from his wrath.

This conversation clearly over, I went to the kitchen pegboard for keys. I'd been given full use of the cars there, which I was taking full advantage of once I changed and could get the hell out of this house.

"You won't need those for school." Dad got the jump on me again, folding his paper crisply before standing. "Hubert will take you to school. He's warming the car now for you."

Hubert was his driver. "How will you get to work?"

"I'm taking the Rolls-Royce," he said, grabbing the driving gloves I hadn't noticed by his own kitchen plate. My dad would have a driver and not even use it. Back before Mom died, he hadn't quite reached the level of success he had now, something he never failed to wave in front of my aunt's face whenever he saw her. She had to work sixty-hour weeks as a nurse to put food on the table. He merely had to make a phone call with a few clients. He grabbed his briefcase. "Have a good day at school and be mindful of your curfew. Things won't be like they were back with your aunt. I have rules here."

He did have rules, didn't he? And what happened to me in LA had nothing to do with my aunt, or where I lived. I was sure he'd never see it that way, so there wasn't a point in defending myself or my geography. My dad had placed me in a tight little box, and as far as he was concerned, that's where I would stay. Also, something told me his sentiment of me "having a good day" was more for formality than anything. I didn't believe he actually cared to wish me well. I was an obligation, his daughter, and he had to say things like that.

He started to walk off but stopped. "Let me know if you hear anything about your sister. You know, kids talking or whatever?"

Yes, I'd definitely tell the one person what he wanted to know about the very reason I stood in this house instead of on the way to my own school. Paige not being here now had everything to do with him and absolutely nothing to do with me.

Dad's lips turned down. "Though, don't you get your hopes up. She's probably dicking around like she always tends to do. She'll make her way back when she feels like it. Have fun waiting around while she gets her shit together."

I'd blanch if this wasn't expected, my sister "dicking around" to the point where even my aunt wasn't concerned anymore. Paige and my dad got into things so much that her just up and leaving had become old hat for years since she came to live with him. It wasn't unheard of for me to wake up with my sister on my aunt's couch or even sleeping in my desk chair after she took a red-eye to get away from him. It also wasn't unheard of for her just to leave town and ghost for days on end after she and Dad truly let into each other.

She just needed space sometimes but she always popped up...

She'd never been gone an entire summer, though.

Two

The school uniform rode up my ass like a son of a bitch, a literal atomic wedgie which I endured the entirety of the trip inside a chauffeured car. Maywood Heights was a smaller city, but not a sleepy town by any means. People were alive and well, maple leaves of gold and umber tones being raked up in yards the size of football fields. What I'd dubbed as McMansions followed one after the other, a far cry from the graffiti apartment complexes and litter-filled streets I came from. I didn't live exactly in the city, a suburb, and people didn't care about their shit like they did here. I had a feeling they might have given awards out for some of this landscaping.

Jesus.

Paige never talked about where she lived much during her visits. Sure, she talked about the basic shit, who she was sleeping with or the crap that went down with her and Dad, but the actual town, not so much. Crossing my legs, I attempted to adjust my skirt again, bracing myself for the day to come. When Paige moved away, we'd been in different grades. I mean, she was a year older than me at nineteen, but her tendencies to miss classes and I guess "dick around," as my dad would say, placed us both as seniors this year. At least, she would have been if she were here. The school had been told about this from what I understood. Though, my dad tended to keep his dirty laundry on the DL. As far as they knew, Paige simply wouldn't be attending school for the time being and his other daughter, me, would be finishing out her senior year here instead.

"Windsor Preparatory Academy, Ms. Lindquist. Would

you like me to pull up right to the doors or is the start of the quad to your liking?"

Passing through gates with a crest comprised of orange and navy sections, another football field presented itself in the form of the quad. These people had a quad, many other chauffeured cars such as mine dropping off students with navy and sun-kissed ties, as well as pleated skirts that rode just as mine. These girls seemed to be used to it, though, the tights. Rosanna actually laid out knee-highs for my ass, but I wasn't having that. Putting up with nylons, I adjusted those, directing Hubert to take me to the main doors. The other kids seemed to get out early to meet each other for a longer walk, and hiding like a little bitch gave me time to gawk at them a little behind tinted glass.

What have I gotten myself into?

My plan was simple, be here and make myself known until my sister rescued me. She had a tendency of doing that, playing savior whenever I needed her. There's a reason she'd been so quick to leave with Dad, take the brunt of his parenting and keep the focus off me, and I wasn't unaware of the sacrifice she'd made all those years ago. Her dealing with our strict and sometimes cold father meant I never had to. She'd been there for me by ironically leaving me, so if I came here and word ultimately got back to her about it, she would be back.

She always showed up for me.

Hubert stopped in front of the large oak doors, and after handing me a bag filled with books, he directed me to see the headmaster first. There, I'd be told my schedule and instructed where to go. Basically, the baby bird would be thrown right out of the nest and into the prestigious halls of Windsor Prep.

"Your father instructed me to give you this card as well," he stated, handing me plastic over the seat. Black and heavy, the credit card already had my name on it. Hubert formed a smile behind a gray mustache. "For your lunches."

And I'd be sure to load it up with lots of Pop-Tarts and sugary crap. Just because he didn't want it in his house didn't mean I couldn't keep a few boxes in my locker.

"Thanks, Hubert. And for the ride."

"Of course. I'll be here when you get out. Two thirty on the dot."

I nearly made the man promise this, to save me from this place and what used to seem like a smart decision. Frankly, my sister would kill me if she knew I was at her school living with Dad. She really did always try to keep her life with Dad as separate as she could from me. I'd never been to visit her. She always came to me before I could, holidays and everything. When I did see my dad, it was because he came along for the ride. We really were the epitome of a "happy" family.

Gripping my bag, I scaled brick steps that matched the buildings situated in various sections of the quad. Students ventured to all facets of the place, but I'd been told the main building positioned at the center was where I needed to be. The fact that I didn't have to bypass security and metal detectors floored me upon entry of a building that smelled uniquely rife with age and upper class, and following the signs, I easily found the headmaster's office.

I think the large gorilla head had something to do with that.

I'd read the school's mascot was "The King" in the pamphlets Dad gave me to prepare, but seeing the motherfucker straight on was a sight. It bared sharp white fangs like actual King Kong, a mock growl at anything that dared to pass its bust. The headmaster had it on a column before his office, and I was sure the life-size version dancing on the football field in a felt costume did exactly what these people hoped it would to anyone going against them in a game. It was truly terrifying, giving me chills as I shook my head and passed. Inside, I was told to take a seat, and eventually, the school's headmaster, Principal Hastings, did see me. It took a sec. Apparently, he'd been in meetings most of the morning according to his secretary. By the time he saw me, I'd been more than ready to get this show on the road, shaking his hand and letting him welcome me into the institution. It was the traditional song and dance of a new student coming to a foreign school, but I'd honestly been surprised the person at the top of this place had to do something so arbitrary. I supposed the alumni dollars may have required it, so I sat for the introductions and, later, the handoff of my schedule. It was nothing fancy considering the grades I brought in here, and I was sure Dad had to make a couple phone calls just to get me into the place. I didn't consider myself dumb by any means but I was sure the public school curriculum was leagues behind the place that sported King Kong as its mascot.

"We're happy to have you here," Principal Hastings concluded with, placing his hands together on a wide oak desk. "Though, we were very sad to see Paige won't be joining us this year. Have you heard anything different about her?"

A town this size and school this elite, I wasn't surprised he'd heard about my sister going AWOL. He was probably one of many I'd hear either asking or whispering about her whereabouts in the days to come.

I opened my hands. "Your guess is as good as mine." Besides a few texts here and there at the beginning of the summer, I'd heard nothing from my sister, absolutely nothing, and I seemed to be the only one who worried about that. My sister may have had bouts of acting out, but never had she gone such an extended amount of time without word. Especially when it came to me. I shrugged. "I'm hoping with me being here she may come back."

This really was the plan. Places like this talked, people busybodies. She'd hear I was around.

At least I hoped.

Principal Hastings said nothing to that, simply nodding when he stood. "I hope you're right and she really will be missed around here in her absence. You'll be sure to let us know if you hear any changes?"

I told him I would, and after a quick shake, our meeting concluded with him escorting me out of his office. I was told I'd have a guide coming for me to take me to class, and he waited with me for a moment before excusing himself.

"I'm afraid I have another meeting, but you should be all right?"

I nodded as I would, but before he darted off, he waved a finger by his nose.

"This will have to be removed before you start your day, I'm afraid," he stated, referring to my nose ring. "We do have a strict dress code here, yes?"

I'd popped the hoop in outside of the scrutiny of my dad and in the privacy of a chauffeured car. Apologizing for the error, I removed it, and Principal Hastings left me to wait for my guide standing next to the scarier-than-shit simian bust. The King was giving me the eye like nothing else, and the urge to smoke hit me like a freight train.

Shit.

I usually only did weed when I was stressed and I was damn stressed. I figured I'd at least wait until lunch and bop off somewhere, but this guide was taking too long and I needed a smoke. After a quick scan of the halls, I decided to take the map Principal Hastings gave me along with my class schedule and find some place to hide and light a joint. My travels took me outside, and it was like God was looking down on me because the bell signaling the end of class sounded and the sudden crowds allowed me to blend in. Eventually, I peeled off from the packs of students and escaped behind the administrative offices. The back of campus had an outlook of the water, a little lake of some kind, and venturing, I noticed a moderately sized shack. Considering everyone else was headed in the opposite direction, I darted inside the shack and internally screamed sweet relief to find myself alone.

The place was a boathouse. I mean, stacks upon stacks of what appeared to be long canoes were stored on elevated shelving and I touched one. Obviously, this school had some kind of rowing team as well, and I took advantage of the fact when I decided to light up my joint amongst the clusters of boats.

Damn, did I need this.

I allowed the drug to filter through me as I took a seat in a boat aisle. Using my backpack as a pillow, I lay on it, crossing my ankles and watched as my smoke drifted, then clouded toward the top of the house.

I closed my eyes, feeling the release of the drug before a rustle behind nearly made me drop the joint.

Shit.

I started to put it out but stopped at the sound of a little whimper. Getting on my knees, I followed that sound to another aisle and alarm hit me at the sight of a pair of little eyes underneath a boat. I lowered, and when those eyes turned out to be puppy dog eyes surrounded by dark chocolate fur, alarm instantly shifted to warmth. A puppy, a real live puppy, was under there, and getting closer, I made out the breed, a dark Labrador. I had a friend who had one once, and I recognized it easily.

I reached for it. "What are you doing here?"

Friggin' cute as hell, the little guy or girl crawled right into my palm, no more than teacup-sized. Pressing him to my chest, I studied to see if he was hurt since he whimpered, but got nothing but licks to my fingers.

"You must have just been lonely, huh?" I asked him,

smiling as he pushed his head into my hand. Whatever bothered him before he seemed to be okay now. Standing, I considered a game plan for him, but I lost the thought at the sound of moans.

And two bodies.

One in particular was on her knees, a girl with bright red hair as she bobbed back and forth. I saw her easily between the spaces of several boats ahead, and cradling the puppy, I pretty quickly made out who exactly she bobbed back and forth *on.*

He stared right at me, a sandy blond with electric green eyes and a grin for days. He grinned at me, cradling this girl's head while she sucked him off right in front of me. He so obviously knew I was watching, cocky about it. He merely tipped his chin at me before going back to the redhead, those eyes of his falling back into ecstasy, and disgusted, I stepped back. The puppy wriggled in my hands, and completely thrown from what I'd just seen, I accidentally let it loose.

"Hey, hey!" I whisper-shouted, chasing it through the house. I lost sight of it between two boats and cursed before giving up and going back for my bag. I managed to avoid the couple the second time, but I did hear a groan as I made my way back to the boathouse doors.

I slammed it shut behind me, hoping I scared the shit out of whoever they were, whoever he was.

Arrogant ass.

The fucker actually grinned at me, my head shaking as I returned to the quad and went back to the administrative building. I returned to the simian bust, and when my name was called, I turned.

An extremely tall girl made her way down the hall, like the playing-basketball kind of tall. She had dark hair she hiked in a ponytail and didn't wear a skirt and heels like I did. She wore white basketball shoes with pleated pants, and

I had a feeling any skirt they gave her might ride worse than mine.

"Sorry I'm late. You're December, right?" she asked me, waving. She had a few books in her hands, a smile on her face. "They just told me I'm supposed to take you to class."

I wondered at the "they" but figured she'd misspoken since Principal Hastings was only one man. I lifted a hand. "Yeah, that's me and no problem. I haven't been waiting long."

Technically, this was true considering my little detour. Fighting myself from cringing at the show before, I shook the tall girl's hand.

"I'm Birdie Arnold," she introduced, and I smiled, loving her original name. I hadn't heard that one before, cute. She grinned. "I'm a senior like you. You ready for class? It's mine too. Second period English."

Happy to at least know one person, I followed her across the quad to our English class. The class had already started, but I think the teacher, Mr. Pool, had been warned about my arrival, so he didn't give us a hard time about it. He introduced me to the class of about twenty-five or so, then Birdie and I took seats off to the side. The room settled for about two seconds before the door opened again, and a familiar face sauntered himself into the room, looking thoroughly satisfied with his chiseled jaw and thoroughly tousled hair like he just had a round in the sheets. Who knew what he and the redhead did before I got there.

His strands of spun gold complemented a clean-shaven face. This guy's cheekbones could cut glass and I think he knew it. Stopping the class in conversation, he came fully equipped with a note folded between two fingers, one he passed off to Mr. Pool without breaking his stride.

"A late pass from the headmaster," the guy informed, that smile of his hiking before he ventured to the back of the classroom. Pulling off his blazer, he exposed a set of chiseled biceps and similar forearms when he rolled up his sleeves. He concluded by loosening his tie. Second period English was apparently this guy's relaxation period. Once he finally made it to his seat, he clasped hands with not one but several guys in the back. Those who didn't get handshakes got fist bumps, and Mr. Pool merely shook his head at the spectacle.

"I'd expect nothing else, Mr. Prinze," he said, huffing before tossing the pass on his desk. "If you're done?"

Mr. Prinze gave him the floor, nodding like he led the class instead of the teacher. What was laughable was Mr. Pool actually let him do that before going to the board and bullet-pointing today's lesson.

I pulled my English book out of my bag. "I just saw that guy," I whispered, getting Birdie's attention. Mr. Pool's back was still to us, and Birdie turned, looking to the back of the room before facing me.

"Royal?" she asked. "What was he doing?"

That guy's name would be Royal Prinze. His parents were probably pretty damn impressed with themselves too. It all seemed fitting, though, considering the way this boy owned second period English.

Lowering, I explained to Birdie quickly what I saw in the boathouse. Mr. Pool was still busy at the board, and once my story concluded, Birdie did nothing but smirk.

She lowered too. "I'm not surprised, but I'm sure you know all about that, him."

"If you'd all turn to page ninety-seven, and we'll begin our look into the Renaissance period. December, I'll touch base to see where you are in your studies later, but don't be afraid to let me know while we work today if you're lost or anything, all right?"

The attention on me, I pulled away from Birdie and what she said. Giving Mr. Pool a wave, I told him I would, and he gratefully moved on but not without me catching the eye of a certain green-eyed blond. He had his legs crossed, thick and muscular, in my direction. Pen to his lips, he flicked at it with a finger, making a silver ring flash on his right hand.

"Why would I know about him?" I asked, purposely severing his connection with me and talking to Birdie.

She frowned in my direction. "Royal Prinze?" she questioned, to which I shrugged. She tilted her head. "He's only your sister's best friend."

Get on Amazon today!

Printed in Great Britain
by Amazon

46999475R00155